THE TROPHY WIFE'S USER GUIDE

L. BETH CAMPBELL

The Trophy Wife's USER GUIDE

KNIGHTS

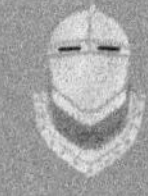

KNIGHTS

L. BETH CAMPBELL

Erica, thanks for listening when I rant about trick plays and bad calls while watching football

I GUESS that it shouldn't surprise me that I ended up here, exactly where I wanted to be. In fact, this is everything I've worked my whole life to achieve. I'm standing in a million-dollar mansion in a gated neighborhood among the wealthiest people in the Kansas City area. A couple million dollars here will get you more bang for your buck than it does in many of the other cities in the United States. With his work schedule and the square footage, we could theoretically live separate lives, only crossing paths when sharing a meal. No one ever warns you that having a bigger house without people to fill it merely means larger spaces for the loneliness to settle when you decide to keep others at arm's length.

The diamond on my left ring finger catches the light refracting from the crystal chandelier in the home office as I search for the binder. I could have sworn I'd locked it in the bottom drawer, but it's not where I last remember seeing it. If he found it, he'd be smart enough to piece it all together. It was shortsighted of me to leave it anywhere he could read it. If he knew what I had done, it could mean the end of this new life of mine. With the way the fans would react, this could mean the end of any chance for me to have this again.

I THINK my fate was sealed on the day that my mother gave me a name that means "wealthy." It's strange how similar "Odette" can sound to, "Oh, debt." While my mother refuses to disclose the identity of my birth father, I know that he was a professional athlete. My mother was a cheerleader—beautiful, but underpaid. She loved her job and the attention she got from the professional basketball players on the team. Though he was once very interested in my mother, he was decidedly uninterested in being a father. He contributed financially and genetically before turning his attention to "other interests." Being a single mom didn't mesh well with her former job as a cheerleader for a professional sports team. I think part of her was sad to lose both him and her dream job. The financial security helped her get over the heartbreak.

Maybe the force that turned me onto this path had something to do with the prestigious private schools and boarding schools my mother sent me to. I had to earn good grades to ensure scholarships, but every phone call home contained a lecture about the value of networking with my wealthy peers. When dealing with generational wealth, connections are more important than net worth. In the world of business, connections are how you close deals. Your qualifications will only take you so far unless you have the relationship currency to buy your way into new social circles.

Somewhere amid all the crazy boarding school drama, I found a friend. More than just a best friend, I found a sister. During my freshman year at boarding school, Natalie was my assigned roommate. Her father owns the largest retailer in the country, making her family part of the 1%. We instantly connected as we shared everything. Natalie is one of the few people who understands my ambitions and dreams. Because of her social status, I've been able to get into exclusive parties and events just by being with her. The only unfortunate part is that she doesn't have a brother as a dating option.

All the boarding schools and academic achievements were to ensure my spot at an Ivy League university among the richest and brightest. Yale University featured the same vibes and many of the same crowds of rich kids that I had experienced in boarding school. Natalie and I shared an apartment right outside the campus. While my undecided major for the first two semesters might have indicated to some that I lacked focus, it was quite the opposite; I knew exactly what I wanted to pursue. I just didn't think it would happen overnight or this late into my 20s.

College was where most of our friends gradually began to pair up and make plans involving extravagant weddings and au pairs. Some matches were subtly orchestrated by their parents and grandparents, but others occurred naturally due to proximity. Natalie and I somehow graduated without boyfriends or fiancés. At least we had each other as we moved back to the city that had been her early childhood home and headquarters for her family's wealth.

Though it started as a cow town, Kansas City has a rich history of political ties to the mafia during the times of the American Prohibition. The river and the train station provided the Italian mob with the transportation necessary to disperse alcohol and increase their fortune and foothold in the city. Natalie cannot confirm nor deny whether her family may have had ties to the mafia in the past, but like the city's government, all her father's business dealings are above board now.

While I had known that Natalie's family was wealthy, I hadn't accurately pictured the kind of house her family owned. The house is in its own incorporated community that's both private and gated. The quarterback for the Kansas City Knights professional football team built a mansion in the same village. While not all the houses are large enough to contain an indoor basketball court, her family's plot of land is one of the largest. Natalie and I temporarily moved into her parents' guest house while we searched for apartments in the downtown area.

She pulled some strings and wrote a check to win us one of the coveted luxury penthouse apartments in the downtown loop. Thanks to her family's generosity, we moved into an apartment approximately the same size as many suburban houses in the metro area. She subsidized my portion of the rent, refusing to take my money. I don't know how to refuse her continual generosity without causing a rift in our friendship. Besides, who would be crazy enough to say no to living with her best friend in her fancy penthouse? It's not New York City or Los Angeles, but Kansas City has its fair share of trendy restaurants and wealthy bachelors.

Those who score the best deals in their industry are well-connected and do their homework. When I'm not working for the ad agency that hired me because Natalie's cousin is on the executive board, I'm doing my due diligence. I have a list of every eligible bachelor on each of the city's professional sports teams along with their current contracts and bonuses. I keep a list of every trendy restaurant, club, and bar in the city with locations and hours. My planner is filled with dates outlining each scheduled concert and venue. It's a compilation expansive enough for a travel blog, but when paired with the written advice from my mother, it's a roadmap to permanent financial security.

My mom did well for herself with the money my father sent, but it's nothing compared to how well off we could have been had they gotten married. She taught me how to be smart and independent. She also taught me that while marrying for love can be satisfactory, marrying for money is more than merely a means to an end.

RULE #1

When a rich man offers to buy you a drink, always say yes

My eyes are closed to focus on the rhythm of my movements and the steadiness of my breathing. Gabe only has two volume levels—loud or silent. "Faster! Keep going, keep going! Push a little bit harder!" He's the right level of infuriating in moments like this. I open my eyes to glare at my personal trainer standing beside my treadmill. "Just a few more strides!" Someone ought to teach him how to use his inside voice. The others in the gym are used to him by now, but his intensity tends to scare off newcomers more times than not.

By the time I've reached the end of the workout, I'm exhausted from the pace and incline challenge. I say, "Sometimes I wonder if you're trying to kill me."

Gabe rolls his eyes and says, "But it's always worth it. You just beat your personal best."

Arms crossed in annoyance, I say, "I would hope so. Otherwise, everything I pay you to be my personal trainer would be a waste."

"You could always take me up on my offer to train for a half marathon," he hints as he has at every training session for the past month.

"You, of everyone, know that's the last thing I'm aiming

for," I say shrugging. "Excelling in sports is irrelevant to what I want to achieve."

With a hint of flirtation, Gabe says, "You know, you should let me take you out tonight to celebrate your reaching another goal."

He doesn't often try to flirt with me, but when he does, it makes things awkward. I remind him, "Gabe, you know that I can't. Plus, I already have plans with Natalie tonight."

"I will never understand your obsession with dating deep pockets," he says as he brushes off my rejection. Gabe will undoubtedly find another girl who will gladly go out with him tonight.

"Don't take it personally. I have ridiculously high standards that the 99% can't reach." I decide to change the topic for both our sakes. "Anyway, thanks for fitting in this last-minute session."

Nonchalantly, he says, "Hey, I can't say 'no' to the birthday girl."

"And here I thought you had completely forgotten."

STILL IN MY workout clothes from the gym, I unlock the front door to the apartment I share with my best friend. Natalie is tall and willowy with proportions suitable for a ballerina. Though she loves to dance, she does not love the damage ballet causes to her feet. She shifted her creative focus to high-end art and interior design instead of pursuing her childhood dream of dancing for a professional ballet company. Usually, she dresses business-formal with her straight dark hair cascading down her back. Tonight, she perches on the couch in clothes that can hardly pass as clothes while scrolling through her phone. When she hears me, she looks up from the screen.

"Please tell me you're not wearing that to the club tonight," she says as she takes in my tank top and yoga pants ensemble. "It's your birthday, and many cute, rich guys will be there tonight."

With an eye-roll, I say, "Of course I'm not wearing this tonight. I just got back from training with Gabe."

It's concerning how much her face lights up at the mention of my personal trainer—concerning because Natalie could be with anyone she chooses, but she seems to harbor a crush on someone who has yet to make a move. "That boy is too hot for his own good. If he weren't so obsessed with you, I'd totally date him."

Once again, I roll my eyes at her statement. I tell her, "He is not obsessed with me. Maybe you should let him know you're interested." With her looks, brains, and money, there's no way Gabe would pass on the opportunity to at least go on a date with her.

"Too much work. I prefer that they come to me," she says and shrugs. "Go shower and I'll pick out some acceptable options for tonight."

I follow her orders and head to my shower to rinse the sweat from my workout. Although I'll likely be covered in sweat and other things in a few hours, I need to feel clean until then. I keep my time under the running water to a minimum before wrapping myself up in a towel. Natalie makes quick work of finding outfit options between our two closets.

Tonight is more than just my 27th birthday; it's also a chance to finally be noticed by guys who fit my particularization. What I wear tonight could make a difference in whether or not I can get a date by the end of the night. Some people find their matches on dating apps, but a dating app isn't likely to tell me whether a guy is wealthy enough to support my ambitions and ideal lifestyle.

Usually, Natalie's fashion taste is excellent enough to pay for her services, but when it comes to nightclub attire, I question her sanity. All the shoe options are heels that scream, "You're going to have blisters tomorrow!" Sore feet are a small price to pay for the boost they give to my appearance, though. I'm unsure why she owns so many crop tops and mini skirts and how she has three of each in my size. She and I share the same shoe size, but we are not the same body type. I opt for the scarlet-themed ensemble, leaving behind the sequins and leopard print options.

Despite that they're my size, the clothes are tight. I quickly apply makeup that will be a pain to remove when I'm dead on my feet later tonight. I inspect my reflection and remind myself that rich men can't see my personality and brains from across the room; they can only see my looks. My looks are the bait that will set the trap. Satisfied with my appearance, I walk into the living room where Natalie has returned to her social media scrolling. I clear my throat to catch her attention.

She looks at the finished product of her wardrobe choices and says, "Now that's more like it. Guys won't be able to keep their eyes off us when we walk in."

"That's because I'm barely wearing any clothes," I point out. Even though I'm dressed, the style makes me feel like I'm showing a lot of skin. I'm not lacking in the area of confidence; however, common sense tells me that the air outside will be colder by the time we leave whatever venue Natalie has chosen for the night. I brush off my concerns for later and hype myself up.

Natalie says, "As my mother always says, 'If you've got it, flaunt it.'" I roll my eyes at the overly used idiom.

With a hint of sarcasm, I say, "Funny, your mom sounds exactly like mine." My phone starts to buzz from the cross-body clutch holding my phone, ID, and credit card. I pull it out and see an incoming call from my mother. "Speaking of the devil..." I answer because she'll keep calling until I do. It's not surprising she waited this late into the day to call me on my birthday.

"Happy birthday, baby girl!" My mother's voice is cheerful on the other end. I can faintly hear the background noise from whichever Hollywood set she's working on tonight. "I'm sorry I couldn't spend this one with you."

"Thanks, mom! I understand that you had to work. I've been pretty busy today too." A work deadline was the only thing that kept me from taking the day off. Even if I had used my PTO, I would have spent the majority of the day alone until my session with Gabe at the gym. My mom works in the hair and makeup department for various Hollywood studios. Whenever she's scheduled for a big-time movie, that takes priority over anything else. Her job might pay well, but it's not always a stable income.

She says, "I hope you've been busy with staying focused on the plan and not getting distracted." Ah, that didn't take her long. I roll my eyes at her comment, thankful she can't see my face. Only my mother would deem my full-time job a "distraction" from what she believes I should be doing instead.

"Mom, you don't have to remind me. Natalie is taking me out to an exclusive club tonight." That alone is enough to both appease her and hint that I can't talk on the phone long. Since she's still at work, this conversation will end sooner rather than later.

"Well, remember our rules for going out," she says, ignoring my earlier statement about not needing reminders.

Exasperated, I say, "It's hard to forget when I've been reciting them since I was three."

"Okay, well, have a good time, and good luck tonight," she says, finally taking my hint. "Just remember, the pretty bait catches the expensive fish."

I'll likely strain my eyes by how much I've been rolling them today. Between my mother and Natalie, I can't catch a break. The voice in my head doesn't need their help. "Bye, mom."

I take a deep breath to calm my annoyance before looking at Natalie and saying, "Let's go before all the good guys are taken."

To this day it still amazes me the doors that open just by saying the name "Natalie Cornwall." Not only is she recognizable at the most exclusive country clubs in the city, but she also skips the line at clubs and concerts with her name. Kansas City doesn't have many celebrities besides professional athletes and a few artists and actors, but her family's reputation spans generations. Somewhere in her family tree, a Pendergast married a Cornwall.

"The bouncer didn't even check for an ID," I shout as the neon lights and pulsing music engulf us. A Friday night at the end of summer is peak business for venues such as this one. When I see how many people are inside, I understand the line outside the building.

Natalie says in my ear, "Either my family is more famous and influential than I thought, or he was too busy checking you out to think of anything else."

I laugh at her statement. "I should have known you'd use my lack of clothing to your advantage."

There's a mischievous expression on her face as she says, "Trust me, give it thirty minutes and it'll be to your advantage as well. My intel told me that some of the Knights players are here tonight. Should we get drinks first or join the dance floor?"

"I prefer staying sober for the time being so I can properly assess the men here," I say. My decision not to drink earns one of her eye-rolls.

"You and your rules," she mutters, but I still catch it over the volume of the music.

Since it's my birthday, she goes along with my wishes and follows me to the dance floor. The thumping music is almost overwhelming, but the high energy of the club equalizes the intensity. While the dance floor holds some potential prospects, I know the cream of the crop is likely at the bar this early into the night.

Even from here, I can recognize the faces of some of the wealthiest bachelors, but one in particular catches my eye.

Liam Cartwright is a professional football player for the Kansas City Knights and one of the best tight ends in the league. I can't say for certain that it's him, but I know the chances are very high, especially if that's Arthur, the star quarterback, with him. The two share a strong friendship that translates to game-winning chemistry on the field. One of the local grocery store chains features them together in advertisements, and a few of Arthur's other endorsements have started utilizing their bromance in ad campaigns.

I keep the two football players in my line of sight as I tell my best friend, "Nat, you were right about some of the Knights players being here. I think that's Liam Cartwright and Arthur Welch over by the bar."

"Did you really doubt me?" she teases as we continue to move to the beat of the music.

Though I'm subtle about keeping my eyes on them, it's obvious when Liam has noticed me. I can feel the heat of his stare despite the crowds of people around us. "Should we go over there and introduce ourselves?" I ask her.

"I don't care how many millions of dollars they make or how many thousands of yards they run, that outfit is too sexy for you to have to make the first move. Just give it a few more minutes." I follow her advice; as usual, Natalie's instincts are correct.

I watch from the corner of my eye as Liam and another Knights player who had just joined him at the bar make their way over to the dance floor. He's several inches taller than the average man, putting him a head above the others as the sea parts to let him through. He's much larger in person than he seems when I watch him play on TV. As he draws closer, I don't hide that I've been watching his trek across the room to talk to me.

"Hi, gorgeous," he says, and it's jarring how a stranger's voice can be so familiar. That's the bewildering effect of talking to someone who's essentially a celebrity. I've watched him play football and listened to his post-game interviews, but we still don't actually know each other. "My name's Dalton, and I've been trying to gather enough courage to introduce myself."

Oh, he is definitely Liam Cartwright. He's in too many advertisements for me to mistake him for anyone else. I have doubts about whether pretending to be someone else like that works. I'm not sure what his endgame is, but I'll play.

I flirt back, "Well, I'm flattered. I'm Odette."

"Odette...beautiful name for a beautiful girl," he says only loud enough for me to hear. The way he purrs my name sends shivers down my spine, but I manage to keep a poker face. Neither of us will be giving away our hand anytime soon.

Despite my stoic expression, he senses how my body reacts to my name on his tongue. "Odette, can I buy you a drink?"

Rule #1: When a rich man offers to buy you a drink, always say yes.

Knowing that I have him exactly where I want him, I say, "I would love that, but only if you tell me more about yourself."

I half expect him to lead the way as some guys tend to do, but Liam gestures for me to walk in front of him. His chivalry catches me off guard for a moment, but I recover and walk toward the bar. Due to his stature and confidence, the crowd automatically parts for us as if he were Moses at the Red Sea. I order a strawberry daiquiri and water to offset the dehydration and sugar from the drink. I can't hear what Liam orders over the bass drop, but the bartender hands him what appears to be a piña colada. We sit in silence for a moment while I take a moment to look at him up close.

Without the millions of dollars he makes from his football contract and endorsements, he's still a catch. Liam is tall and muscular with dark hair, bright blue eyes, and a neatly trimmed beard. During the earlier years of his career, he was depicted as a talented player on both the football field and in the dating field. He's 30 and has yet to "settle down" in the way many other players have. His best friend Arthur is my age, married to his high school sweetheart, and has two children. I didn't see the young quarterback leave, but he's no longer at the bar or on the dance floor. Natalie is dancing with the other player—one of the starting wide receivers—who had been at the bar. Knowing that she can handle herself, I turn my full attention and energy to the large presence beside me.

I can tell that every word and every subtle touch is intentional, clearly communicating his motives. It's disconcerting how easy it is to be myself around him. As much as I want to play hard to get, my resistance is wavering. Between the daiquiri and the electricity in his touch, I want to give in to his charm. I refuse to order more than one drink because his presence is intoxicating. Liam can give me everything I have been working towards, but it will only work if I maintain control of the situation. I'm certain that our flirting chess match has reached a stalemate until he discharges his secret weapon.

I know it in the seconds before it happens as he leans in closer, those azure irises fixated on my lips. He kisses me like he knows exactly how I want to be kissed. It's so passionate and so consuming that I nearly forget where we are and who we are. I've never experienced a kiss that made me forget everything important to me. I let myself want him because he's the type of man I've been aiming for. And just like that, I'm his, but he's just as entangled as I am.

I ignore the stares, glares, and judgment of other women as Liam leads me onto the dance floor. Those women all think that I'm a gold digger for setting my sights on someone who makes millions. Those women are correct in their assumption, but I would argue that their assessments are hypocritical. They all want a chance with him for the same reasons I'm dancing with him right now—possible fame, wealth, or both. Yes, he's also attractive. Most women aren't going to be petty over a man who's attractive and poor, though. They claim they don't care about money, but the majority would give a chance to an unattractive millionaire. If you find someone who's both, you do what's necessary to lock it down.

As we dance and flirt, Liam looks at me the way the love interest looks at the girl in romantic comedies. I could ignite under that gaze if I were the type of girl to obsess over those things. He doesn't have to tell me that I've got him where I want him.

"I'm going to check in with my friend and run to the restroom, but I'll come find you," I tell him as I reluctantly leave the warmth of his proximity. Natalie follows me to the line outside the women's restroom. Architects never design enough restrooms for women to keep up with the demand. Fortunately, the queue moves faster than expected. I finish before Natalie and wait for her. When she comes out, she looks like she's done for the night.

"I'm ready for a hot shower and my bed, but you should stay here with Liam," she says with a small smile. "Turn on your location sharing and let me know when you're on your way home or if you need a ride. I know he's had a bit of a reputation in the past; however, he's been more levelheaded in the last few years. Don't be afraid to tell him 'no' if he asks for more than you're comfortable with. You won't hurt his ego or his pride."

"Nat, I'm a big girl who can handle herself," I remind her as I pull out my phone to share my location with her.

As soon as I'm back in the main room, his eyes lock with mine. He stands at the bar with a glass of clear liquid in his hands as he hits me with his smile. I smile back and walk toward him, inwardly scolding myself for melting at the sight of him.

His size should mean he has a higher alcohol tolerance than the average, but no sober man would have ordered a limo to pick us up from a club at 1AM. Yet, here we are in the back of a limo as his lips find mine over and over again.

When he says, "We should elope," I know he's anything but sober. This isn't Vegas where there are chapels with Elvis impersonators ready and waiting for poorly-thought-out decisions. Kansas City has its fair share of casinos, but it likes to give off the vibes of being "wholesome" despite historical ties to the mafia and the popularity of modern-day breweries and distilleries. If there are 24/7 wedding chapels with celebrity impersonators in this area, I've never heard of them.

"How are we supposed to get a marriage license when the courthouse is closed?" I ask out of curiosity. While marriage to someone rich has always been my endgame, it's shocking how easy this seems to be. I've always assumed I would have to learn how to survive his games, practice schedule, and the media well before a proposal was on the table. He doesn't even know my last name yet, but he's asking me to take his.

"Don't worry. I know some people," he says with the full confidence of someone who is a famous athlete. I should talk him out of the inane idea, but I can't help but wonder how and if he could pull off a wedding tonight.

"I'm not sure if I believe you." Multiple phone calls and an hour later, we exchange vows in full regalia with a marriage license from the state. We've both pulled off the impossible tonight. Our marriage is too rushed for a prenuptial agreement, a detail that will make my mother proud. I come down from the adrenaline rush on the drive to his house. Neither of us has the energy to do anything but change out of our clothes and crawl into his fancy bed. It's so comfortable that I sleep like the dead.

"Where am I" and "What am I wearing" are the first two questions that float through my mind as I drift awake. Sunlight peeks through the crevices of the blinds on the opposite side of the room from the bed. The shadows are all wrong for this to be my room. Last night's events crash hard enough to give me mental whiplash. I met Liam Cartwright at a club Natalie took me to for my birthday. In a whirlwind romance, we got married on the same night we met; however, I don't remember doing anything more than kissing. I was tired, but I'd had all my mental capacities. I did manage to change into a T-shirt he gave me to sleep in.

This is the part I hadn't thought through when I agreed last night. Soon, he'll wake up, and there's a very legitimate chance that he'll regret everything he did last night. He might not regret talking to me or kissing me, but marriage is a big commitment that most take more than five minutes to discuss. Plus, he didn't even get the whole "wedding night" part of the deal since we fell asleep. In addition, he's mildly famous. His life is private enough that he doesn't have to deal with constant paparazzi, but his name does end up in the tabloids and on gossip sites. He has an agent and publicist who would have to deal with the fallout were the news of our quickie marriage to make any headlines. I decide that the best course of action is to leave a note so that I can go back to my apartment and shower. Natalie is likely worried that she hasn't heard from me.

"Leaving so soon? I thought that maybe you'd want to have breakfast before starting your day." His voice startles me when I try to grab my belongings. I could have sworn he was deep in sleep only seconds ago.

"I should probably let Natalie know that I'm okay," I explain. His eyes are still closed when I turn around to look at him.

"Well, at least take a shower first and drink something before you leave," he says and opens his eyes to look at me. "I've got a great shower, top-of-the-line espresso machine, and all the ingredients for protein-packed pancakes. I think Natalie will be less worried if you're clean and well-fed when she sees you."

I almost miss his reasons for why I should stay a bit because those eyes capture my attention all on their own. He does make a good point about the food. My issue is having something clean to change into after I shower. I don't know whether my stay will work in my favor when it comes to the elephant in the room. As if sensing my hesitation, he offers a solution. "I can have my assistant go out and find something for you to change into. In the meantime, I have a few extra robes you can wear. I'm afraid most of my clothes will be too big for you due to my height."

"You're making it impossible for me to leave right now," I say as I walk toward the open door to his bathroom. "I can stay for one hour, but after that, I really should go back to my apartment." I flip the light switch to one of the most pristine bathrooms I've ever seen. As I walk past the mirror, I catch a glimpse of my reflection and wince. Between the exhaustion and not going home, I hadn't taken off my makeup last night. It's a wonder that he looked at me the way he did only moments ago. I can tell which sink he uses based on the toothbrush and face wash. He's left a clean folded towel by the other sink for me. Did he do that last night, or had he gotten up earlier only to climb back into bed to sleep more?

The rain shower system quickly warms up, and I relish the feel of the water gliding down my skin. What I wouldn't give to get to use this shower every evening. It's a step above the luxury of the downtown penthouse apartment. I use the time to mull over ways to broach the topic of our marriage and my desire to make it work. We have to make it work long enough that an annulment is no longer on the table, and I have to convince him that it's not fraud on my end. The wedding was his idea, after all, even if he was too drunk to remember it.

Besides his masculine body wash, the shower has plain bar soap. It's gentle enough to use on my face to scrub away what's left of last night's makeup. Due to my usually stringent facial care routine, my face is still pretty without the extras. I don't mind letting Liam Cartwright see that side of me if it'll help my case at breakfast. The white fluffy robe reminds me of the robes at all the spas Natalie has treated me to in the past. I would forget clothes if I had a way into my apartment without being seen by the public. This is a robe I could live in forever.

Thanks to the shower, I feel remarkably at ease and ready. That is until I hear a knock at the door, and Liam walks in wearing only a towel.

"Where are your clothes?" I ask him, failing to hide my flustering.

He shrugs and says, "I took a shower in one of the other bathrooms. My closet is off this bathroom and I didn't want to disturb you while you were in the shower."

"How considerate," I say sarcastically. Liam disappears from the bathroom without my notice as I attempt to untangle my mess of hair. My curls are at the point of no return; the only thing that will save them is a wash and condition.

The smell of pancakes leads me through the hallway to the kitchen where my clutch sits on the island. I have no recollection of this room last night, but we must have come through here on the way to the bedroom. The kitchen, living room, and dining area have an open floor plan with windows letting in natural light. While the floors are stained dark wood, the walls are a soft white that brightens up the space. He doesn't have much in terms of decorations, but he does have furniture that wasn't bought from IKEA. It's a bachelor pad of the highest quality with the potential to be more.

Liam stands at the stove in blue sweatpants sans shirt. Does he usually cook for his dates shirtless, or is this just his normal when he's at home? Is this something I'm expected to get used to if we stay married beyond today? Though he senses my presence, he waits until he finishes the pancakes to say something.

"The espresso machine is on, and there's already milk in the attachment," he says as he grabs toppings for the pancakes from the fridge. "It's all automatic and fairly simple to use."

I press the selection for a cappuccino, and the machine does everything from grinding fresh beans to frothing the steamed milk. Natalie has one similar to this in our apartment, but his machine appears to have more bells and whistles. He pulls out plates and silverware and gestures for me to help myself. His options are on the healthier side, which I recognize because I tend to buy the same brands. He has the only brand of syrup I've been able to find that doesn't have high fructose corn syrup listed as an ingredient. It's still sugar, but it doesn't seem as overbearing as some of the other types commercially available. I pile a third of the fruit on the pancakes and drizzle my plate with syrup before taking a seat on one of the island barstools. Liam does the same while his coffee brews before sitting next to me.

"We didn't do anything more than kiss last night, right?" I ask to break the silence. I'm nearly certain that we didn't, but I don't know how much he remembers from our spontaneous night.

"Are you asking if we slept together or are you gauging whether I forgot about our wedding?" Well, at least he's direct. "Even if I'd blacked out that part of the night, I woke up with a wedding ring on my left hand and a gorgeous girl in my bed. But no, we didn't sleep together. You would remember if we had."

My entire body blushes at his last comment as I say, "You're right. I would remember if my first time had been with Liam Cartwright."

The man beside me freezes mid-bite as he stares at me. I knew telling him like that in that manner was a bad idea, but my big mouth went rogue on that one. It's not something I'm ashamed of in any way. Unlike other girls, I didn't date around or hook up with guys in boarding school or college. I refused to let myself be vulnerable in that way with anyone.

"I didn't realize that you're a virgin," he says once he's recovered from the shock. "Most girls your age aren't, especially when they look like you. Not that you look like you sleep around a lot—you're insanely beautiful. Any guy would be an idiot not to try to pursue you. When did you realize who I really am?"

Last night, this man oozed charm and irresistible confidence, but my confession has him flustered in a way that's atypical for him. "I knew right away because I've seen your face everywhere in this city. You're essentially a celebrity. But you clearly didn't want me to know, so I thought I'd play along."

"I guess we both could have been more truthful with each other," he says sheepishly before checking the notification on his phone. He gets up from his chair and walks to his front door. A shopping bag sits on his front porch.

"I should change and go. My phone died at some point last night, and Natalie will file a missing person's report if she doesn't hear from me soon."

Liam looks at the time on his microwave. "I would drive you there myself, but I need to check in to the training facility today. Football season is only a few weeks away. Coach will have my head if I skip out today. Let me have my assistant drive you to your place. Then, she can help you pack whatever you need from there."

Pack?

RULE #2

When executed properly, a gold digger in the present is a trophy wife in the future

HE WANTS me to go to my apartment and pack. I need to be sure I heard him correctly. "What am I packing for?"

He looks shy as he says, "Sorry, I just assumed that you would be moving in since we're married. Maybe we should talk about it since the whole thing was rushed, but I don't really have time to stay and have that discussion right now. My assistant will drive you and give you my phone number. I'd love to take you out to dinner tonight if you don't have any other plans."

"Dinner sounds nice, but it sounds like I might be busy moving," I say as I smile at my husband who seems to want to stay my husband. There has to be a catch somewhere, but I'll go along with it. Catches are how he makes his living, after all.

"We can always order in, or I can cook," he says. He kisses my cheek before he grabs his keys and walks in the direction of what must be the garage. I hadn't even noticed when he had cleaned up our mugs and plates, but the dirty dishes were nowhere to be seen. That man is a walking distraction.

I navigate back to his room to change into the clothes his assistant had dropped off. The outfit is simple—a KC Knights

T-shirt and a pair of high-quality leggings. There's even a pair of sliders so I don't have to put my heels back on. The simple gold band on my hand feels foreign and unlike the ring I'd always imagined I would have. I never dreamed I would marry someone less than twenty-four hours after meeting, either.

Fully dressed, I walk to the kitchen where a woman who appears old enough to be my mom is helping herself to the espresso machine. When she sees me, she says, "Hello, I'm Liam's assistant, Helen. Just let me finish making my coffee, and I'll be ready to take you to your apartment."

I awkwardly stand and wait, unsure of how to respond. She's not what I pictured when he mentioned his assistant earlier. I had imagined a girl around my age who may or may not be secretly in love with him. This woman could be his mother, not that the age difference matters to some people.

"I'm also his mom, in case you were wondering," she says in a way only a mother could. Now, it makes sense. While the familial relation eases my worries about his agent possibly harboring feelings for him, it's unclear how much she knows about her new daughter-in-law. Does she know the extent of her son's escapades last night, or does she assume that I'm his new girlfriend or one-night stand?

Realizing that I haven't introduced myself, I say, "I'm Odette. I appreciate that you're willing to give me a ride to my apartment."

"Of course, dear," she says as she grabs her travel cup from the espresso machine and switches it off. "Liam doesn't need me to drive him around much these days, and I miss trekking my boys to and from practices and games like I did when they were younger."

Liam's younger brother Lance was a top-tier cornerback in college but chose not to pursue playing professionally afterward. I know that having that knowledge makes me sound like I'm a stalker, but I honestly just enjoy football. If it's on

Wikipedia, it's not a secret. Liam's mom being his assistant is not something you'll find on any online informational sites.

I follow Helen into the garage where she's parked. She walks to the driver's side of a red Tesla and gestures for me to sit in the front driver's side. It's a higher-end model, of course. In my experience with those earning millions, they either have too much money to care about their car's gas efficiency or they're willing to pay for a luxury EV to avoid going to the gas station. Depending on how many millions they have at their disposal, they can have both. Some like to collect classic cars or other expensive things. With one glance around the garage, I see that Liam has three cars he keeps at his house, assuming that he drove one to the training facility.

It's awkward riding in the car with Helen because I'm unsure of how much to say. A girl likes to be warned before she meets her mother-in-law. Preferably, a girl would meet her in-laws before the wedding. She's going to be upset that she missed the wedding of her firstborn, and the blame will fall on me because he's her son. How am I supposed to pack my things and explain why this morning is the first time we're meeting?

"Are you usually this quiet, or did I take you by surprise by telling you I'm his mother?" Helen asks to break the silence. "I may not always agree with my son's choices, but he's an adult. I raised him not to be stupid. Any misgivings I have about this particular decision of his has less to do with you personally and more to do with his lack of planning or forethought. He's never been this impulsive before, but he's been under a lot more pressure lately from both the team and his publicist. Either way, I'm willing to give you a fair chance. You have to let me get to know you, though."

Does that mean she knows the full extent of her son's impulsive decision? My mother's advice was lacking in terms of how to handle his family members; she focused more on the lead-up to marriage than on the things that come with it apart from the money. I know I'll have to call her to tell her the news at some point. That's a conversation I'd like to have later rather than sooner. For now, I can put my best foot forward with Helen.

"I share an apartment with my best friend," I say. "She and I met in boarding school and went to Yale together. She's how I ended up moving to Kansas City. Her family is from here."

"Where were you from before you went to boarding school?" Helen asks, showing genuine interest. "And how old were you when you started? I didn't realize that people still send their kids off to school before they're 18. I know I wouldn't have trusted my boys before that age."

"I was born in the Portland area, but we moved to LA when I was five. I was twelve when I started boarding school. My mom still lives out in LA. She works in hair and makeup for movie sets."

She deliberates over my brief answers for a moment before she asks, "Is your father in the picture?"

"My father was never in the picture," I say politely since it's all I care to disclose to her at the moment. His absence doesn't affect me now the way it did when I was younger. I've never even asked my mother for his name or contact information. Helen is understanding of my answer. Though she never filed for a divorce from her husband, the two have been separated for years. If I knew her well enough to ask, I would inquire about whether they intend to reconcile at any point.

"Liam's dad comes to nearly all his games," Helen says, assuming that I'm aware of their situation. "He didn't want Liam to play professionally, but ever since Liam was drafted, he's put in effort to be supportive. The stubborn man refuses to move to Kansas City to make it easier; I might consider giving him another chance if he ever sells that old house to be closer to his son."

"I don't think there's anything that could convince my mom to move away from Los Angeles," I share.

Helen Cartwright is a talker, filling the conversation after asking her questions. When she pulls into the garage for my apartment complex, she asks, "Do you want me to come up with you? I can also stay here if you need a ride anywhere else. Let me give you mine and Liam's phone numbers."

My phone has enough of a charge that I save their numbers. "I have my own car, so I shouldn't need to take up more of your day." Her expression is one of disappointment, which is why I add, "But if you want to come up, I just need a few minutes to talk to my roommate first."

Helen brightens at my offer and parks her car in an empty spot. She follows me into the lobby where she sits to wait for my text. I like Helen, a feeling that exacerbates my guilt over marrying her son for his money. She doesn't treat me like she suspects I'm a gold digger.

When I unlock my door and walk into my apartment, Natalie is sitting in the same spot where she had been waiting when I came home after my gym session yesterday. Her welcome is infused with sarcasm. "Oh, good, you're alive. What happened to you last night? Did you spend the night with Liam? I thought you turned on location sharing, but your phone hasn't updated your location since two in the morning."

"My phone died," I start in explanation. "By the time I started charging it, I knew that it would be better to explain my whereabouts in person."

"Were you with Liam?" Nat asks again.

"Yes, but I promise it's not what you suspect," I say and sit next to her on the couch.

Natalie's eyes drift down until she spots the ring I forgot to take off. Her eyes widen as she points to the simple jewelry. "When I left you, you weren't drunk enough to make that kind of stupid decision."

"I wasn't drunk, but I can't say the same for him," I hedge as her face lights up the moment she puts the pieces together. "He's the one who suggested that we get married. I didn't have it in me to try to talk sense into him since it's exactly what my end goal was. I half expected him to demand an annulment as soon as he realized it this morning. Instead, he suggested that I pack and move in with him. He asked me to dinner tonight. Oh, and his assistant who is also his mom gave me a ride here. She's waiting in the lobby and wants to come up to see the place."

Natalie reaches for my phone and says, "I'll text her right now to tell her to head on up." My best friend loves meeting new people no matter how awkward the circumstance is.

"I'm not sure if he's told her the full extent of our relationship. She seems nice, but I can't imagine that she would be thrilled her oldest son married a girl he just met last night. I'm hesitant to tell my mother for the opposite reasons."

"You've accomplished everything she could have ever wanted for you in much less time than you thought possible," Natalie says admiringly. "Before his mom gets here, I need you to tell me how he was in bed."

I had hoped the impromptu wedding would distract her from that question. "We fell asleep as soon as we got to his house. So technically, the marriage hasn't been consummated."

"You might want to get on that so he doesn't change his mind," Natalie says calmer than her usual tone. "You'll be sharing a bed for the foreseeable future. My advice is likely unnecessary given the way he looked at you last night. In case you didn't catch my meaning, I'm officially kicking you out unless you two split up. When do I get to meet him properly?"

"Soon, hopefully. I was already going to move out without your permission."

"I always knew that you would land here one day, but I did not expect it to be today. The one time that you do something out of character for you, and you finally got what you've always wanted." Natalie's observation brings out the irony of the situation. My research hasn't been completely useless, but it hasn't been as helpful as I assumed it would be.

"I feel like I'm in over my head with all this," I admit for the first time.

"If anyone can handle something as crazy as this, it's you," Natalie says reassuringly. "And I can tell by the way that Liam looked at you that he's already crazy about you."

I shrug off her compliment. "Something about it just feels off. What if this is too good to be true?"

"You're just nervous. You need to embrace your new amazing life as Mrs. Liam Cartwright." We both stand up when we hear Helen's knock at the door. I open the door for the woman whose opinion can make or break my future. She glides in with the pose of a woman who's used to luxury without being entitled to it as she scopes out the apartment that's been my home for the last few years. Natalie and I are both good about keeping our apartment clean, and I silently thank my past self for making sure everything was picked up and put away before leaving for the club last night.

Natalie holds out her hand and greets Helen, "Hi, I'm Odette's best friend Natalie Cornwall."

Helen's face lights up with recognition at hearing Nat's last name. "Well, if you're related to the Cornwalls that I'm familiar with, it would explain how you scored such a beautiful apartment. This view from your living room is spectacular. Can I get the official tour?"

Those six words phrased as a question are some of Natalie's favorites. She would give our other friends a tour each time they came over if it weren't overkill. It goes hand-in-hand with her love for interior design and art. The Cartwrights are new money from Liam's successful career in professional football. They were your typical middle-class family in the Midwest. Now, his notoriety outside football is gradually expanding. Eventually, he'll have to make serious plans for life after retirement from the sport. Unless he's one of the exceptions, he'll only be able to play at a high level until he's 35 or 40.

I sit in the living room and wait until Natalie and Helen return. The two laugh and joke as if they were old friends rather than strangers until ten minutes ago.

"You should join us for a spa weekend sometime, Helen," Natalie says in her easygoing manner. "There's nothing like a good, long massage to make you forget about everything else."

"Liam is always getting onto me about not taking enough time off for myself," Helen says and shakes her head. "I went to Paris for a whole month at the beginning of the off-season. Now that is a great place for a girls' trip." All my international trips have been with Natalie as her guest. Although she always insisted on paying my way, I felt as if I were taking advantage of her generosity. Somehow though, I don't think I'd feel the same if Liam were to whisk me away to any of those destinations. It's different when you're married to the person who insists on spoiling you.

On a normal timeline with a planned wedding, we would have left for our honeymoon today. It hasn't hit me until now that a honeymoon trip won't be possible for a while with football season approaching. Preseason games begin in August, regular season in September, and playoffs in January. Ever since Arthur became the starting quarterback for the Knights, the Knights have had more success in the postseason than at any other point in the team's history. Instead of being disappointed with a loss in the wildcard round, Kansas City has been spoiled with multiple championship wins. If this season is like the last few have been, Liam won't have time to get away until mid-February. By then, we'll know each other well enough to decide if a future together is still something we want.

Helen stays for about half an hour before she excuses herself to run some personal errands. Today should be her day off, I would guess. I assure her that I'll let her know if I need anything before I walk her to the front door of the penthouse. Once she's gone, I retreat to my room to start packing up the life I had until last night. It's a wonder that anyone moves with how much stuff we tend to accumulate by staying in one place. I should have asked Helen to bring me plastic containers and boxes. In the hours that pass, I fold and roll and rearrange all the clothes Natalie bought for me without my asking. I'm nearly satisfied with my packing job when I remember Liam's dinner invitation for tonight.

Do you still want to go out for dinner? I have my things packed, but it's going to be an ordeal getting this down several stories and loaded into my car. I don't think it's all going to fit.

With how hard he trains, he's going to need to be fed before I ask him for the physical labor needed to get all this to his house. I shuffle through my dresses until I find the one suitable for most of the fine dining restaurants in the city. My phone dings with a text alert as I fish out a pair of heels.

LIAM

I just made a reservation for Bristol Seafood Grill. We can get your stuff after we eat. Just tell the hostess you're with Liam Cartwright when you arrive.

What Liam doesn't realize is that he's chosen a restaurant close enough that I can walk there from the apartment. It'll make it easier for our post-dinner task as well. I text him a confirmation and get ready for my date. Our first date. Even though we're already married. My phone lights up with a text from my mom asking about the club last night. I leave it unread because I don't know how I want to respond to her yet. Telling her everything isn't something I want to worry about for now.

Natalie is in the kitchen cooking dinner for herself when I

walk out of my room. She whistles at the ensemble that she likely funded.

"Are you staying in tonight?" I ask. Natalie typically prefers going out on a Saturday night, but everyone needs a break from the nightlife on occasion.

"Yeah, I have a huge week coming up, so I'd rather start it off well-rested," she says. "Where is he taking you for dinner?"

"Bristol," I say. It's one of her favorites. "Afterward, we're going to move my stuff out. I'll officially introduce you if you're up for it."

"Of course, I'm up for it. Just text me when you're on your way up." She returns her attention to the chopped onion and garlic simmering in the frying pan on the stove.

I take the short journey down the elevator and to the restaurant to meet my husband. The hostess brightens when I mention Liam's name, and she gingerly leads me away from the main dining area. When I round the corner to the private table, Liam sits in a suit. The velvet red box is a stark contrast to the white tablecloth. He stands to pull out my chair for me and to push it in after I'm seated. Once he sits across from me, he slides the box to my side for me to open. I look down at the ring, only to be blinded by the iridescent light. The diamond is large enough to pay for a whole year's tuition, and the setting is exactly what I would have chosen.

"Is this real, or am I still dreaming?" I ask in shock.

He flirts, "Would you like me to pinch you?"

"Yes. No. Maybe." I'm unsure of anything at this moment with the gemstone blinding me. Liam laughs at my reaction before he leans in to kiss me. There's a table between us to keep things from becoming too steamy, but the sparks are undeniable.

"Dreaming?" Liam asks as he pulls away.

Dazed, I say, "That felt pretty real." Real, while also too good to be true.

Liam takes a deep breath as if preparing to give a speech.

If he hadn't just given me a ring, I would be concerned for our immediate future. "Look, I know this is a big shock, and it was clearly very rushed. If you want to get an annulment, I completely understand."

"Does this ring mean that you don't want one?" I ask to be sure of his intentions.

"Drunk or sober, I married you because I wanted to," he says sincerely. "There's something special about you that I want in my life. Despite our circumstances, I don't regret that decision."

This is everything I've ever wanted, everything I've been working toward. After one night that seems like destiny, I'm married to one of the top football players in the professional league. I've already made it further than my mother did with my father.

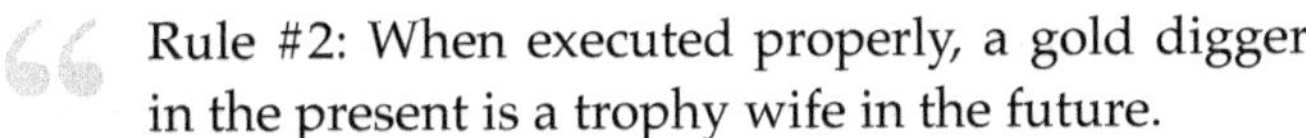

Rule #2: When executed properly, a gold digger in the present is a trophy wife in the future.

"Liam, this whole thing is obviously new to me, so it's a bit overwhelming," I admit to him. "But if I'm certain of one thing, it's that I have feelings for you. As unconventional as it is, I think we owe it to ourselves to try this." Despite my ulterior motives, my confession is true. I take the ring out of the box and slip it onto my left ring finger.

"I should warn you now that once the season starts and I'm in the spotlight again, it won't be easy for you," he says with a hint of concern in his voice. "As soon as the media catches wind of my marriage, it'll be all over the tabloids and gossip sites. People are going to try to find out whatever they can about you. Some will present you in a positive light, but they're going to look for dirt. Arthur has been with his wife since high school; that hasn't stopped the hundreds of women online who accuse her of being a gold digger. It'll be worse for you if you don't develop thick skin."

This is one arena where I'm perfectly suited to be the wife

of Liam Cartwright. I've spent my life as the odd one out, the "poor kid" among the kids of the one percent. Other girls constantly accused me of befriending Natalie for her money. The term "gold digger" is far from new to my ears, and at least this time, the assumption will be correct if I can even hear it from Liam's private temperature-controlled suite at the stadium.

"Liam, I'll be fine," I tell him. "It takes a lot to hurt my feelings, and I've never paid attention to the opinions of strangers. The only opinion that matters is yours…and maybe your mother's. You should have told me that your assistant is your mom before you left me alone with her."

"Is it weird that I keep her role as my mom and her role as my assistant in two different boxes in my head?" Liam asks in a way that explains the missed communication. "She uses a different phone number when she's on the clock to help separate the two roles. I can see how that would catch you off guard, though. Next time, I'll warn you before you're about to meet one of my family members. I can promise you that I'm not related to my publicist or my agent."

It's a good sign that he works with his mom well enough that they know where to draw the boundaries. The boundary I'm most concerned about is the one I still don't have an answer to. "Does she know about the wedding?"

"Yes, I told her that we got married on a whim," he says with a sigh. "She handled the news fairly well, all things considered. She hides it well, but I know she's disappointed that she missed out on being there. We may get roped into having a ceremony and reception for my family once the season is over."

"I like that idea," I say. My mother would like that too. And Natalie. I should see if I can talk my husband into a destination wedding. Arthur and his wife got married on an island during the off-season a few years ago.

Liam insists that I order anything and everything that I want, and I do as I'm told. I listen to him share about training camp and the other guys on the team. He tells me about the pranks going on this season, the rookies showing the most promise, and the schedule they have for the next two weeks. The playing time on live television is only a fraction of the life of a professional athlete. The more he explains, the more it makes sense that his mom is around so much. Many of the other players have a partner as their support system through the toughest parts of the job. None of them could do it on their own.

He glances at the check the waiter brings, but only to calculate how much he wants to leave as a tip. Some players are rumored to be stingy despite their millions. Liam leaves twice the amount I spotted on the bill.

"My apartment building is on the same block as the restaurant," I explain to him as we walk out hand in hand. His large hand engulfs mine. He follows my lead, focusing on me instead of the people around us who recognize him. No one would ever mistake him for a Dalton Nobody. He doesn't let go of my hand until I need to unlock the door to the pent-house. Liam whistles at the view of the city lights through the large windows in the living room.

He says, "If I didn't need somewhere with privacy, this is where I would want to live. Maybe I should try moving in with you and your roommate instead to see if it's feasible." I can tell he's joking by his goofy expression.

"Holy diamond!" Natalie exclaims before I've had the chance to introduce her to Liam. She lifts my left hand to inspect the diamonds that glitter even under the dimmed lights of the living room.

"Hey, Nat, this is Liam," I say and gesture to the towering man behind me. Her eyes scan his body in a way that would bother me if she weren't my best friend. No, it still bothers me, but much less than it would if any other woman looked at him that way.

"Signed, sealed, and delivered!" She exclaims to him once her gaze returns to the ring on my hand.

Liam says, "Well, I liked it, so I refused to let Odette be the infamous Beyonce song." And there it is. I roll my eyes at their ridiculous song references. Once again, Natalie gets along with a Cartwright. This time, though, it's at my expense.

"And here I thought we could have a normal conversation," I say to poke fun at the two of them.

"I think you two abandoned normal when you decided to get married before the first date," Natalie points out and winks.

"To be fair, I kissed her before the first date, too," Liam says, earning a light punch from me. With the types of hits he's used to taking, even my heavy hits would be light to him. Fortunately for him, I'm right-handed, so my punch wasn't with the hand wearing the large gemstone that could do damage. That wouldn't be a healthy way to start this relationship.

"Odette has a lot of stuff for you to carry, so I should let you get to it," Natalie says to excuse herself. I slip off my heels and lead Liam to the pile that I wasn't exaggerating about in my text to him earlier. Without my heels on, he seems like a giant standing next to me with his nearly six and a half feet of height. Tight end is not a position filled by someone short.

When he sees the mountain of my personal belongings, he says, "It's a good thing I brought the SUV with a large trunk. I'll never understand why women have so many things."

"Coming from the guy who has thousands of dollars in football equipment. Do you think that we women just wake up looking like this?" I gesture to my face to reiterate my point.

"Unlike most women, you don't need all that to look beautiful," he flirts, but it's sincere in a way that incites my blush. He shrugs off his suit jacket as I slip on a pair of sneakers. "So, are you ready to load all this up and go home?"

Home. I've lived in many places, but I can't remember a

time when somewhere truly felt like home. All my living arrangements have been temporary. It's hard to believe that this won't end the same way. You see, my whole life I was taught how to attract rich men and the steps to become a trophy wife, but never did any of it give me practical advice on what to do once I became one. I was out of my element, waiting for the carriage to revert to a pumpkin.

RULE #3

Like all guys, rich men love a good pursuit

I TYPE his address into my GPS in case we get separated as we make the drive from downtown Kansas City to the suburb of Leawood. While there are plenty of cars on the road, it's nothing compared to how congested the highways can be during rush hour. One of the benefits of living downtown was taking the streetcar to work. I'll miss the ease of taking public transit as my commute. Except, do I have to work anymore? Do I want to work anymore? Does Liam have assumptions or expectations one way or the other?

Now that we're on the same page about moving forward in this marriage, he and I need to discuss expectations. If he wants me to travel with him for road games, I'll have to take time off. My boss may not be lenient enough to allow me the flexibility for eight weekends, but my boss is a big Knights fan. Private seats for a game or two could sweeten the deal when I talk to him. Before, I assumed that I would put in my notice at my job as soon as I reached this point in my plan. Looking at the metrics, quitting right after a quickie wedding is too obvious. Liam might even question my intentions if I behave too much like a "trophy wife" too soon. I don't mind the idea of working while he's at training camp during the day, anyway.

Either Liam is a cautious driver, or he's purposely going slower to help me tail him. I appreciate it, although, I don't need it. It might not be Loch Loyd, but his gated neighborhood provides all the privacy he could need. Paparazzi aren't common in Kansas City, yet it's better to be on the safe side. Arthur originally purchased a house that was easily accessible to the public. Most in the city will treat players like normal people; they will also casually drive past their houses if they know the address. It's an unusual dichotomy. With every football championship ring and increasing endorsements, Arthur and Liam have crossed the threshold to the tier of celebrity status. With great recognition comes greater security measures.

I follow Liam until we're at his house. Before I can turn off my car's engine, Liam opens the driver's door and gestures for me to climb out. Once I'm out, he folds himself into the seat to program my car's garage door opener with one of his garage doors. I've never lived anywhere I've had to use it before now. Instead of trying to safely drive my car inside without moving the seat back, he clambers out to let me do it. My car is cheap compared to the other makes and models housed in Liam's garage. He doesn't seem to care. I'll know if my intuition is correct on that if a more expensive car takes its place in the coming weeks or months.

Liam closes all the garage doors to keep out the bugs so he can prop open all the interior doors leading to his bedroom. A house of this size and layout should have several extra bedrooms, but it's assumed we'll share. We shared a bed last night without any issues. He unloads my car first.

"I'll carry your stuff in while you get an idea of where you want to put it or how you want to organize it," he says after I move in my first load. "You might not be able to get it all put away tonight or even in the next week, but you'll want to have it done before the first week of the regular season. Once the games begin, it's the last thing you'll want to work on in your free time."

If it weren't already late, I would try to knock it out in one night just because he doesn't think I can. He's right, though; I need a plan on how I want to organize before I can start putting things away. Liam's giant walk-in closet is the stuff of daydreams. It's a room in and of itself with decorative overhead lights, dozens of drawers and shelves, and an ottoman in the center. Though Liam wears his jerseys on the field, the players wear tailored suits when flying to road games. It's their runway during the season. Because of his penchant for fashion, Liam's clothes claim more space than the average man. Due to the size of the space, half of it sits empty and waiting for my wardrobe.

Liam walks in carrying my oversized suitcase like it weighs nothing. He whistles while he unloads all my stuff wherever he thinks is the most useful to me. He isn't even breaking a sweat carrying it all. He's used to the weight of 300-pound men tackling him; helping me move is a walk in the park. I decide to start with my fall and winter clothing since those are the seasons that are approaching. While Taylor would never let me leave the apartment in anything that looks cheap, my clothes seem lackluster compared to what I've seen Arthur's wife Jen wear to games. As much as I would love a shared credit card with the Cartwright last name etched across the plastic, I can't ask for it this early in the game.

"Remind me in the morning to get you a key and security code for the house," he says on one of his trips inside.

"Waiting until the morning so that I don't have the option to sneak out tonight?" I tease as I open the container he set down moments before.

I thank my past self for having the forethought to neatly fold my sweaters when packing earlier. Now, I can arrange them easily on the shelves, lining them up by color. I'm so engrossed in the organization, that I don't notice Liam sitting on the ottoman watching me.

"I really want to kiss you, but I know I'll break your

concentration and workflow if I do," he says in a low voice that invokes goose flesh on my arms. He's right; if he kisses me, I won't get anything else done tonight in terms of unpacking. It was easier to ignore the electric tension when he moved in and out of the house, but now it grows thicker with each passing minute. Even though we haven't known each other long, he's my husband. It's normal to want to kiss my husband more than I want to unpack. I choose to finish my sweaters before doing anything rash.

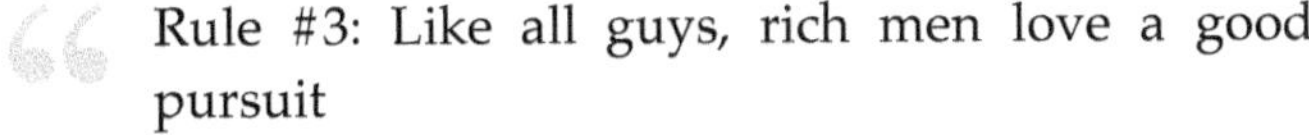

Rule #3: Like all guys, rich men love a good pursuit

When I'm satisfied with that section of my half of the closet, I confront the heated gaze that's been focused on me. With just one raise of my eyebrows, he stands and walks until he's standing in front of me. He's a breath away, but he refuses to touch me without explicit invitation.

"Are we going to address the elephant in the room?" I ask him with my eyes locked on his. The depth of his blue irises engulfs me.

"Babe, there's a whole herd of elephants in this room," he says without a hint of sarcasm. "We'll be up for days if we try to address each one of them tonight. Is there one in particular that you would like to tackle tonight?"

"With the way you're looking at me, my virginity is probably the one we should discuss." He breaks eye contact and shakes his head with a small smile.

He leans in to whisper in my ear, "As long as you don't intend on staying that way while married to me, I don't see how it's an issue. All you're doing is delaying the inevitable by bringing it up."

I refuse to be the one who cracks first, but his statement turns me into a puddle. Somehow, I'm still standing and breathing. I refuse to admit to myself that I'm equally thrilled and afraid of what comes next. Afraid *because* I am thrilled.

Wanting too much of him and from him puts me in a place where I'm not the one in control. But is the one who's in control here the one who holds out or the one who chooses to break the barrier?

We both win and we both lose as our lips and bodies collide and tangle. We kiss like we're starved and craving the other. It's what our wedding night should have been on a normal timeline or even at a normal time of night. His kisses are words that communicate things neither of us want to admit like "I've been waiting my whole life for someone like you." All of it was inevitable.

HE SLEEPS DEEPER than anyone else I've ever known as if he's exhausted and his every desire has been satisfied. If I were capable of loving a man without considering the financial gain or loss, maybe I could love a man like him. I haven't seen him at his worst or in any stressful situations yet, so it's up for debate. This is the honeymoon phase where he looks at me like he can't believe I'm real. If he had seen and known all the pieces that make me who I am, he never would have approached me at the club. No man intentionally marries a gold digger while he's young and has options.

I reposition myself in his arms before letting the weariness of the day overtake the parts of my mind that want to over-think what we just did.

"IF YOU DON'T HAVE ANYWHERE you need to be today, we're staying in," Liam says as he draws lazy circles on my arm. "I won't get the chance to take you on a luxurious honeymoon until the off-season, so this is the best thing I can offer at the moment."

"I've heard some people don't go on their honeymoon trip

right away," I offer. "They choose to use the time right after the wedding to get settled and used to being married. Then, they go on the trip months later when the 'newlywed obsession' has faded into everyday life. Makes it easier to enjoy the vacation, I would think."

Liam kisses my bare shoulder before he says, "Is that what this is? Newlywed obsession? I just thought it was marital bliss or one of those overused phrases married people like to use to explain their happiness."

"I don't know," I admit. The downside of spending my life focused on marrying for money is that I have nothing to compare this to. I don't know what it is to be in love with someone or feel the agony of a breakup. Those are experiences I lived vicariously through Natalie.

"On another note, remind me to send a thank you card with complimentary tickets to your personal trainer," Liam teases, and I lightly hit him for the comment. I hadn't even thought about Gabe or our usual early Monday morning session. He's going to flip when he finds out about Liam.

Eventually, Liam rolls out of our warm cocoon to forage for food in the kitchen. I wrap myself in the same robe from yesterday before following him. Based on the number of yolks I count in the bowl, the man spends a small fortune on eggs.

"Is that all for you?" I ask, half joking and half serious.

"I'm not about to let you starve if that's what you're wondering," he says with an unamused expression. I sit on a stool at the kitchen island and watch the flexing of his forearms as he slices peppers and mushrooms to add to the omelets. "Maybe I should have asked you this before I proposed, but do you know how to cook?"

"Yes, but there's a difference between knowing how to cook and enjoying cooking," I say. "I'm surprised you don't have a private chef. Don't you have a particular diet that you're supposed to follow for optimal athleticism?"

"Jeff will be here tomorrow afternoon to go over my goals

and schedule for the season," Liam says as he pours the concoction into the frying pan on the stove. "You're welcome to join us if you want. My assistant will be there, too, since she helps with the grocery shopping and filling in when Jeff is swamped. Some of the other guys on the team also have hired him. Keeps him busy during the football season."

So many things to unpack in those sentences. "Firstly, he's Jeff the Chef?" Liam nods with a beaming smile. "Secondly, I need to go to work tomorrow if I want to save my time off for road games, assuming you want me there—"

"Of course, I want you there," he interrupts. I give him a raised eyebrow to keep him quiet until I'm finished.

"Thirdly, it's throwing me off that you refer to your mom as your assistant. Grocery shopping is something both roles could do for you."

"Is there a fourth point, or can I give my rebuttal now?"

"The floor is yours." The whole house is his, but I won't feed into his ego. I also prefer not to risk his saying something cheesy in return about it being ours now. Our marriage certificate has yet to be recorded at the county courthouse.

"If you hate your job, you have my full support to quit. But if you love it, keep working. My only condition for quitting is that you would have to find something you're passionate about to fill your days, whether it's another job or a cause you want to spearhead. Arthur's wife Jen has her own interests that he supports at the same intensity that she supports his career. That's how Kansas City became the first in the world to build a stadium specifically for a professional women's sports team. Find a passion project, and let me help you pursue it."

A passion project, hobbies, and interests are all things that took a backseat to my constant research on every single heterosexual male in the metro area worth over five million dollars. Then, I had to narrow the ages to 25-40. Kansas City has professional sports teams in football, soccer, and baseball with rumors of possible basketball and hockey teams in the future. The athletes are a percentage of the available pool. Then, with Natalie's input, I kept tabs on which restaurants, clubs, and bars certain crowds were prone to. All in all, my goal to marry rich required a lot of "behind the scenes" work that no one would have guessed.

"I'll keep working for now until I find something else that I want to invest my time in," I say to him as he places one of the omelets in front of me. I slide off the stool to make myself a cappuccino at the espresso machine.

"I could have done that for you," Liam says as he pulls me into his arms. It shouldn't be possible to feel this safe with someone whom I've known for less than a week. Although it unnerves and unravels me, I wait until my coffee is ready to pull away from his embrace. I swap my full mug with an empty one and select his preferred drink. I sashay the few feet to my stool fully aware of his staring.

While we eat, Liam gives me an overview of the regular season schedule with the likely departure dates for the road games. The only one he's unsure of is their international game. Some teams prefer to arrive in Europe as early as possible to adjust to the time zone difference. Others have waited to cross the Atlantic until closer to the weekend without adjusting since the games are scheduled late enough in the day that they would be awake either way. Those games are typically aired around 8:30 in the morning in Kansas City's time zone.

"Do friends and family members usually travel with the team for the international matches?" I ask to mentally prepare myself.

Liam is thoughtful for a moment before he says, "It varies. Jen used to come with Arthur before they had kids, but it's harder for the kids to adapt to the time changes. Even the shifts between Daylight Savings Time and Standard Time can be a nightmare for Jen with the baby and the dogs. My mom will decide based on how long we're going to be there. If there isn't enough time for sightseeing, she stays home and makes sure I come home to clean laundry and food."

"Your mom, not your assistant," I point out.

"I wouldn't let my assistant touch my dirty laundry," Liam says as if that were obvious. "My mom changed my diapers and can't be scared off by my sweaty practice gear. My mom can leave a pan of her homemade lasagna in the freezer for me to reheat after hours on a plane."

"Family recipe?" I ask out of curiosity.

"Secret recipe. She refuses to tell me what the secret ingredient is. Anytime I've come close to getting it out of her, she tells me that I'll have to get married to find out because she's only going to pass it down to a daughter."

A daughter like me? "Except that the type of woman you married would keep it a secret from you just because she could," I say with a mischievous glint in my eyes.

"Don't start a war you can't win. If I discover you've been keeping secrets from me, I know where you sleep. Plus, it's to your benefit to share the recipe with me because I'll make it for you anytime you want." He gradually leans in closer as he makes his case, stopping a breath away from my lips. Liam likes to tease me to see if I'll take the initiative to kiss him first. I lean back and sip the last of my cappuccino. As soon as I set my mug down, he swiftly lifts me out of the stool, carrying me bridal style to his room.

I DIG to the bottom of my suitcase to find my loungewear so I don't have to wear a robe all day. The robe has proven to be too easy for my husband to take off whenever he desires. Liam sings in the shower in the next room while I plan which part of my wardrobe to unpack next. In all his media appearances, no one has managed to catch him singing at any point. I would remember his deep, velvety voice if they had. In the public eye, Liam is known for being loud and energetic.

When he first began his professional career, his temper got him in trouble a few times with coaches and referees. Maturity has taught him how to channel that anger into productivity both on and off the field.

While it's hard to determine whether this side of Liam is who he is when he's home alone, it's calmer than the man on television. I can't imagine that someone could be that full of energy all the time, but I've never been one to commandeer the spotlight. I welcome attention without demanding it.

By the time Liam is dried off, my dresses are on the rack and arranged by color. A few were wrinkled during the move, but it's nothing that my steamer can't fix. Sensing Liam's presence on the other side of the room, I ask, "Do you know where my orange canvas bag is? My steamer is in it, and I want to get these wrinkles out now so that I won't have to worry about it when I need the dresses for something."

Liam scans the room and then asks, "Is that the bag right there?" He's pointing about five feet from me on the other side of my suitcase. Too many bags are still waiting to be unpacked. Satisfied that he's served a purpose, Liam walks back into the bathroom to leave me to my mess. He doesn't return until I've steamed all my dresses.

"Turns out that moving is a lot harder when you have a lot of stuff," I say and plop onto the ottoman.

He hands me a key and asks, "Is there a six-digit number that you prefer to use for your security code? I'll go program it in now in case I'm not here when you get home from work tomorrow."

I text him the code to diminish the risk of his forgetting or mixing up the numbers between the closet and the main security panel by the garage entrance. I slip the key onto my key ring before I misplace it among the bags of clothes and shoes. My husband rejoins me in the closet and sits on the ottoman.

"What do you normally do for fun on your days off?" I ask him, sensing his restlessness.

"Sometimes I hang out with the guys at Arthur's place or

they come here," he says. The man loves to be around people. "I told them that I wanted a full day away from them to give my new wife my undivided attention."

Flattered by his thoughtfulness, I ask, "Did your intentions for the day involve activities outside of the bedroom?"

He rolls his eyes at my insinuation and says, "I thought I could give you the official tour of the house. You've slept here two nights in a row, but you haven't seen any of the house besides the garage, kitchen, dining room, and master bedroom."

"I've seen the master bathroom and closet, too," I argue, but follow him out of the walk-in closet.

While on the ride back to my apartment yesterday morning, I researched what I could on the house. Public records don't reveal much, but I did learn that it has five bedrooms, ten bathrooms, over 8,000 square feet, and was newly built when Liam bought it. Photos and detailed information disappear once a property is no longer listed for sale. He walks in front of me wordlessly until we're at the front door of the house.

"This is the front foyer," he says as he gestures to the room with little more than the front door, a crystal chandelier, and two staircases, one ascending and one descending. "Let's go up the stairs first since that'll be the shortest."

His long legs climb the steps two at a time while I quicken my pace to keep up. The other four bedrooms are all on the upper level, each with their own bathrooms and walk-in closets. Most sit empty, but when he shows me the one that's furnished, he says, "My dad sometimes stays here when he comes to town for games." His dad who probably doesn't know his professional football-playing son now has a wife living in his house.

A house of this size is meant for a family and entertaining guests. Liam takes me to the basement level containing a full bar, small wine cellar, golf simulator, steam room, home theater room, billiards table, and ping-pong table. This must be where the guys on the team like to hang out. We ascend back to the main level to finish the interior section of the tour. The home office is large enough that we could both work in it if we wanted. The family room and home gym both have large windows that look out to the backyard. Through the glass, I eye the saltwater swimming pool beside the outdoor patio and cooking area. The pool even has its own pool house with an outdoor shower and sports equipment storage space. Either my husband enjoys hosting large parties, or he wants a brood of children. Possibly both.

"That concludes our tour," Liam says and dips his toe in the pool. "We could go for a swim after lunch."

"If you want to see me in a swimsuit, you can just ask," I tease while we walk back into the house together. He continues walking until he's inside the walk-in pantry.

"Odette, would you be so gracious as to enrich my afternoon with your body clad in the swimsuit of your choice?"

He carries out a bag of brown rice. I find my spot on a stool at the kitchen island and observe how he sears the lemon chicken and cooks asparagus and rice as healthy sides. In our day together so far, neither of us has pulled out our phones except for when I sent him my alarm code. It's refreshing not being tied to my device, fully living in the moment. Because players can't have their phones during games, Liam is used to going hours at a time without checking his. I constantly used mine for research and alerts on the whereabouts of my potential targets.

"Has your dad told you which games he's planning on attending?" I ask. "If he's going to stay here, it would be nice to know ahead of time. I'm assuming you haven't told him about us yet."

Liam winces at the mention of his father. "That conversation is not going to go over well, I can tell you that. It'll be worse if I don't tell him myself before Mom accidentally spills the beans. It's surprising how much they stay in touch for two people who are separated."

"I think they would get back together if he moved here," I say with confidence.

"Oh, that's another thing that's inevitable," he says with a wink that sends shivers through my spine. "What about your parents? Have you told either of them about me yet?"

"I haven't talked to my mom since my birthday right before we left for the club—"

"Wait, that day was your birthday? Why didn't you say anything?" His interruption is a welcome reprieve to aid in my delay in telling the sordid tale of my biological father.

I shrug as I say, "It wasn't important. It's not like you made me pay for anything that night. I can't imagine that you would have treated me any differently had you known. Back to what I was saying. No, I haven't told my mom yet because she hasn't tried calling since the wedding. She works in hair and makeup for various movies and TV shows in Hollywood, so her schedule is all over the place. It's easier if I wait for her to call me whenever she has a break."

"Is your dad in the picture at all?" Liam asks, bringing it up again.

"I've never met my father," I admit. "My mom has never told me his name, and I've never asked. I think she would tell me if I wanted to know. I do know that he was a professional basketball player for the Portland Pigeons. I could narrow down his identity using math and the process of elimination. My mom was a cheerleader until she got pregnant. He didn't want to be a father at that point in his life, but he helped financially. As far as I know, he's never changed his mind about wanting to keep his distance. My mom's parents helped her out the first few years until my mom and I moved to LA. Then, she sent me off to boarding school, which is where I met Natalie."

"That sounds lonely," Liam says in a way that makes me think he sees me more than I realize. It was lonely until I met Natalie. I love my mom and appreciate all the sacrifices she made to give me the best life possible, but my childhood was lonely once we moved away from her parents. Most kids in my class at school had a dad who was around, even if their parents were no longer married.

I give Liam a small smile. "My mom is going to love you." She's going to love Liam while also lecturing me about keeping my heart and emotions in check when it comes to him. While some people cite money as the reason their marriage didn't last, the wealthy aren't immune to the other things that can destroy a marriage. Liam might be completely invested in making us work right now, but I know better than to believe it's guaranteed we'll stay together.

"We should call her," Liam suggests as he cleans up our plates from lunch. "Before we go swimming. You could FaceTime her to tell her the news, and then I'll join you so I can at least meet her virtually. When she has a break in her work schedule, we'll fly her out here to stay with us for a few weeks."

"I don't know if she'll be free to answer, but I can give it a try. Let me go get my phone."

I walk back to the closet, the last place I remember using my phone. I pick it up from where it sat on the ottoman and unlocked the screen to call my mom. I curl up in the armchair by the window while preparing myself to leave a voicemail. To my surprise, her face appears on my screen.

"I was just thinking about calling you," she says. Her kitchen is in the background. "We got the day off from filming, and I've been trying to catch up on the chores. I can order takeout and food delivery to avoid grocery shopping, but laundry doesn't do itself. What have you been up to today? That doesn't look like your and Natalie's apartment. Where are you?"

I take a deep breath before I tell her the highlights of the last two days. Knowing that Liam could be listening from the hallway, I keep it brief. My mom doesn't seem to recognize Liam's name, but hearing that he's a professional football player is enough for her standards. She'll do her research about his contract and known endorsements as soon as I hang up. "Now, I'm sitting in the master bedroom of his house."

"Our house," Liam says as he walks into the room. "We're married. It's our house. You live here just as much as I do. During the season, you'll be here more than I am." He walks around the back of the chair to put himself in the view of the front-facing camera. "Hi, I'm Liam Cartwright."

My mother is incapable of hiding her reaction. Liam is attractive, muscular, and tall. "I'm Heather, Odette's mom. My daughter failed to mention just how handsome you are. She was too busy talking about your instant connection and the result of that. Most men would have filed for an annulment the next morning."

"I'm not most men," Liam says confidently. "I don't shy from going after something that I want, and I'm confident in my ability to see something of value. I've never met anyone like your daughter. It's still early, but I have yet to find out anything about her that would make me second guess my decision to marry her."

"I like you," my mom says to him with an expression I've never seen on her. "You own your choices and take responsibility for them instead of running at the first chance for an escape. That takes maturity."

RULE #4

Ensure none of his close advisors suspect you married for money

I DON'T WANT to go to work. The move from the apartment downtown to Liam's house means I'll need to leave earlier in the morning than I'm used to. I'm tempted to hit snooze, but Liam gets up and turns on the lights to full brightness. The LEDs are too blinding to sleep with them on.

"You're supposed to be on my side," I groan as I throw the comforter over my head.

"I am on your side," he says as he gently pulls the comforter back to look at me. "You don't want to be late for work when you talk to your boss about the time off you'll need for some of my games."

"What if I just quit instead?" I say with a sleepy smile.

He chuckles and shakes his head. "You are not a morning person, are you? Will it help if I bring your coffee to you to help wake you up?"

"How are you so chipper right now? You're the one who kept me up too late on a work night." He gives me an apologetic look before walking to the kitchen to start the espresso machine. I close my eyes while I wait, willing myself to stay awake.

I sit up when I hear his footsteps approaching. Liam hands me the steaming mug and says, "I kept you up late because I feel like we have catching up to do in getting to know each other. In the future, you might have to remind me that you have to work most Mondays. I've gotten used to having the day off."

"I didn't want to think about work," I say between sips of my cappuccino. "I still don't want to think about work, but I'm going to start getting ready as soon as my mug is empty."

The end comes too soon, but I follow through on my statement. When I'm about to walk out the bedroom door to head to the garage and leave, Liam gently grabs my arm to tug me to him. He tilts my face toward his gaze before it can hit his solid chest. I forget everything when his lips brush mine in goodbye. I'm still in a daze as he delicately pushes me toward the hallway.

"Let me know when you're leaving the office so I can start getting dinner ready," he says right before I'm out of earshot.

Traffic today isn't as horrendous as I'd anticipated, but I know today's commute has no bearing on tomorrow's patterns. It's only been three days since the last time I walked into the office. In three days, my life has changed drastically. The first thing I do when I unlock my work computer is check my boss's calendar for any meetings he has scheduled for the day. It'll be easier to request days off after explaining the situation.

While I feel like a different person, none of my coworkers notice that anything has changed. There's a huge diamond on my ring finger that flashes in the light. No one notices the gemstone.

"Jack, when you have a moment, can we meet in your office or the conference room?" I ask my boss when rushes past me to the restroom.

"Give me five minutes," he says.

Five minutes later, we sit in the conference room as I relay my recent relationship change. Jack doesn't hide his shock at the news of my marriage to Liam Cartwright. I've never been one to share much about my personal life before now. Then, I explain the situation with Liam's road games and taking time off.

"Of course, take whatever time you need for that," Jack says without hesitation. "Football is only a few months of the year, and only half the games are road games. I'm surprised you're even here today now that I know about your eventful weekend."

"I really appreciate it," I say with sincerity. "Let me know if there are any games that you want to go to. I can pull some strings to get you tickets."

Jack beams and says, "I'll let you know my top three before the end of the day."

LIAM'S PUBLICIST Sasha looks like she wants to kill him. Her long fingernails are sharp enough that she could probably do some damage if she caught him off guard. I would accidentally stab myself if I had her manicure. An impromptu wedding to someone he hardly knows isn't a publicist's worst nightmare, but it's in the top five.

"I'm not asking this to be rude or insinuate anything, but Odette, are you pregnant?" Sasha asks as she turns her full intensity on me. "If there's a baby, I need to know now so that we have a plan on how we want to convey this to the public. Pregnancies never stay a secret for long."

"No, I'm not pregnant," I tell her with near certainty. Liam and I have been as careful as we can be. Even if there were, the wedding preceded any activities that would have resulted in a pregnancy.

"Thank goodness," Sasha says before she adds, "not that I would be personally against it if that's what you wanted. Professionally, Liam being off the market is going to send enough shockwaves without adding a baby into the mix. It'll make the story appear more 'whirlwind romance' and less 'shotgun wedding.' The former is much more romantic than the latter."

Liam is at ease as he says, "You told me that I need to work on making my image more family-friendly. A wife and kids fit that picture, do they not?"

Sasha rolls her eyes and explains, "Family-friendly means fewer curse words on live television. It means being more of a role model and less of the grown frat boy persona that some football players give off. Despite what some say, not all publicity is good publicity. While I admit that you've done a great job at following my advice, this could backfire on us with some of the endorsements we've been gunning for. It could also be what seals the deal. My advice is to wait for the public to put the pieces together about Odette. Rather than shout the news from the rooftop, treat it as the private decision that it would be for a normal person. It'll seem more natural that way. Let's approach this the same way we did when you started going to church during the offseason."

"So, we just wait for someone to see us together in public and notice the giant rock on my finger?" I ask, wanting to be clear on the plan.

"Most celebrities aren't the ones who tell the public about their relationships unless it's a publicity stunt or they're so infatuated that they can't keep quiet about it," Sasha explains. "Some intentionally hang out in places where they know they'll be caught to make it more subtle. Often though, the paparazzi catch them in what should have been a private moment."

Liam smirks as he says, "What Sasha is suggesting is that anytime we're somewhere that we could potentially be caught, we should be packing on the PDA."

Sasha rolls her eyes and shakes her head. "Do whatever you're comfortable with as long as you keep it PG-13. Let's move on to the next point in this meeting. Odette, I need to know your family background and personal connections. Tell me your whole life story and include anything incriminating that the media could use against you if they found out. It's always easier to fight these things by being ahead of the game. We're already going to have to deal with critics who will accuse you of marrying Liam because he's a professional athlete. I need you to give me enough evidence to prove them wrong."

Rule #4: Ensure none of his close advisors suspect you married for money

"My mom was a cheerleader for the Portland Pigeons when she met my biological dad who was a player on the team. She got pregnant, but he didn't want to be a father. He helped support her financially for the first year, but I've never met him. I don't even know his name."

Sasha tilts her head in thought as her brain goes through all the possible ways the media could spin the news. "It wouldn't be difficult to find him if you wanted to know. Does anyone outside of your family know who your father is?"

"There could have been people who know that were part of the organization at the time, but I don't know," I tell her truthfully. "Do you think someone in the media could dig up something like that to use against me?"

"Since you're not in contact with him and haven't asked him for money, I don't think the news would come out in a negative light," Sasha says. "Well, I take that back. I'm sure someone out there could do an exposé on how you accomplished what your mother couldn't by marrying an athlete rather than merely getting knocked up. Even that is still somewhat positive though because you married Liam Cartwright somewhere other than Vegas."

Sensing my discomfort, Liam reaches over to hold my hand, giving it a light squeeze. He says, "I'm the one who made the first move, and I'm the one who asked her to marry me. I stand by my choices. I was attracted to her because she wasn't throwing herself at me and carried herself in a way that's different from other women."

"I know that, but all those fans out there buying your jersey and gluing your face to poster boards won't know that unless you make a public statement," Sasha reminds him. "Odette, back to your family. You were born in Portland, I assume. Where does your mother live now?"

"She works in hair and makeup for one of the film and television studios in Hollywood," I answer. "I attended public school until she sent me off to boarding school. I had near-perfect grades and earned an academic scholarship to Yale. My closest friend and former roommate is Natalie Cornwall."

Sasha pauses her note-taking on her phone to look up at me. "Natalie Cornwall as in the daughter of Terry Cornwall, who is part of the Knights ownership group?" Until she had asked, I had forgotten that Natalie's father had an ownership stake in the team. It's not a connection that would have given me many opportunities to meet the players in a way that could get me closer to my goal.

"The same one," Liam answers for me. "Natalie was the one who played a part in how we met."

Sasha schemes while we wait for her to ask further questions. "Yale is good. It means you're smart and motivated. Having a lengthy and close relationship with someone well-known in Kansas City is also helpful. Football fans may not all know Natalie, but they'll recognize her father's name. Our biggest hurdle will be building a timeline for your relationship that doesn't reveal that you married within twenty-four hours of meeting. Marriages are public records on the county website once the certificate is recorded."

"You want us to fabricate a backstory for our relationship?" Liam asks her. To me, that seemed like the obvious part of dealing with the media. "I thought we would just let them put the pieces together about the marriage and leave it at that."

"Sasha, I apologize for my husband," I intervene. "He

seems to forget that even though he's not as well-known as the typical celebrity, there are still plenty of gossip sites publishing articles about his personal life. The lack of paparazzi has him fooled into thinking that his life is more private than it truthfully is."

Liam rolls his eyes as he says, "I'm not a fan of lying to the media. I'd rather let them make their assumptions and theories while I play football and enjoy being married to my wife. I should get a say in how much of my personal life they can infringe upon."

I squeeze Liam's hand in understanding. While dealing with the media is important for his endorsements and investments, his focus is on what happens on the field. But what happens on the field is affected by the other aspects of life. Many players have been suspended due to poor decisions off the field, and those decisions affect the entire team. Marriage isn't something the league has any influence on, but it is something that can affect the league. Certain players have been known to end up with wives who are just as or more famous than they are.

Sasha looks to me for a response. I shrug and look at Liam knowing that his opinion is the final say in this. He's the one who hired Sasha for situations like this, but he's also the one with eight years of experience as a professional athlete. To him, following each other on social media is enough of a digital connection to satisfy the curiosity of the masses.

"For now, we'll table that idea, but let me know if you change your mind," she relents. "Don't be surprised if the media start asking questions at interviews and press conferences when the news breaks. The best scenario would be if they latch onto the love story rather than try to poke holes in it."

It's at this moment that I realize my husband is an optimist. He sees and wants the best outcome, even if it's improbable. While I admire and respect his perspective, I pray this decision doesn't come back to bite us. Sasha lets herself out as

Liam and I clean up the plates from our Chinese takeout. We're both lost in our heads as we maneuver around the other. Between work and the session with his publicist, I'm exhausted. I can tell he's physically spent from training most of the day.

"You should go shower while I put the leftovers away," he says to me. "I showered before you and Sasha got here."

Without a word, I walk away to start my nighttime routine. When I emerge from the bathroom half an hour later, Liam is sitting up in bed and studying plays. This is the side of the game that no one sees. Players spend countless hours outside practices and games memorizing the playbook. Liam is well-known for making things up on the fly, but being able to do that well comes from knowing the offense like the back of his hand first. Then, he reacts in the moment to what the defense does whether it's running the play as planned or creating a space to make himself open for receiving the ball.

He puts his tablet on the nightstand when I crawl onto the other side of the bed. "I've been thinking about having the team and their families over to give them a chance to get to know you before the season starts. That way, you won't be a total stranger to them. Arthur and Jen will especially want to meet you as soon as I tell them."

"That sounds like a great idea," I agree. "We should get full use of the pool before it's too cold outside for swimming." I yawn at the last word as my eyes drift closed.

"I'll check with Arthur and the guys to see if most of them are available this weekend," Liam says as I hear the click from his bedside lamp. Even with my eyelids closed, I can tell the room is cast in darkness.

THE REMAINDER of the week flies by with work consuming the majority of my time. Liam's training days are long and hard, leaving him with little energy once he's home. Rather than order in, I cook on the nights that Jeff isn't here to make Liam a specialty meal. Although Liam doesn't complain about my cooking, I know he would rather cook himself if he weren't physically spent. I'll need to work on Helen to get that secret lasagna recipe from her. A pan of lasagna could last us a few nights of dinner depending on Liam's appetite.

On Friday night, I'm almost asleep and facing the wall when Liam says to my back, "How does Sunday sound for the cookout? Mom can get a bunch of steaks from the store tomorrow, and I'll fire up the grill. Everyone else will bring sides and desserts to share."

"Did you already invite them all over?" I ask, trying to recall if he had told me Sunday was a possible date or if this is the first I've heard about it. Either is possible.

"Yeah," he says. I can hear the slight guilt in his tone like he knows he didn't tell me the plan before now. "If you'd rather not do this weekend, we can postpone."

I'm too tired to think of any reason why this weekend won't work. "Let's do this weekend. Is that everything you want to discuss before I fall asleep?"

Liam kisses the back of my head as he mumbles, "Goodnight."

HELEN IS A TROOPER. In her shoes, I would have had choice words for my son if he had made a last-minute request for one hundred raw steaks and two hundred raw burgers. As she hauls in the meat from her car, I understand the reason for the oversized fridge in the basement. Tomorrow is too soon to put the meat in the freezer. I want to question how Liam plans to grill all that meat tomorrow, but the last time I doubted him, we ended up married at two in the morning. He has a plan that he hasn't told me about, and I'm okay with that.

On Sunday afternoon, Coach Anderson and Arthur show

up an hour earlier than the rest of the team, both with grills strapped to the beds of their pickup trucks. They plan to tackle the burgers and steaks the way they avoid tackles on the football field—as a team.

"Hey, I'm Arthur," he introduces himself. "My wife Jen really wanted to come, but she and the kids have been sick this week and didn't want to spread it to the team. I remember you from the club that night. Liam hasn't been able to shut up about you this week."

"Don't tell my wife how obsessed with her I am," Liam tells him with a light punch to his arm. "That's my job."

Coach Anderson wraps his arms around the two players. When they all stand together like that, you can't tell that they're all larger than average men. Wes Anderson was a professional linebacker in his younger days before he retired and started his coaching career. "It seems that no matter how old they get, I always have to deal with players who spend a lot of time thinking about girls," Coach says. "At least by the time they're adults, it's usually the same woman from day to day. I'm glad Liam finally has someone to keep him in check."

"Don't listen to anything they say about me," Liam faux whispers as Coach Anderson releases the boys to move the grills around to the back patio. Wes has three things that are important to him—football, family, and food. Helen is ready with the steaks and burgers, experienced from her years as a mother to two boys.

Within an hour of setting up, our house is full of conversation and laughter. Without their jerseys, I have a harder time telling some of the players apart from one another, but they're all patient with me as I learn their names and faces. The wives, girlfriends, and children add another layer of difficulty. When he's not absorbed in his role as the "grill master," Liam stays by my side with his hand holding mine or around my waist. All of them welcome me as the newest member of their football family.

"I was beginning to wonder if that boy would ever settle

down," one of the wives says as she sits in the chair next to me. "Lately, he hasn't been dating much at all, but maybe maturity made him picky. Seems he found what he was looking for."

"I can understand being picky," I say to make conversation with her. I think her name is Mikayla. I might not be certain about her name, but I do know that she's married to Demetrius, the offensive left tackle. I also know that she's pregnant and about halfway through the pregnancy.

She gives me a sly smile and says, "As you should be. Some women get frustrated because they lose sight of what they should be picky about. I met Demetrius in college. I can't imagine how hard dating must be for people out working full-time. Liam is lucky he found you before some other dude snatched you up."

"Sometimes it's less about luck and more about shooting your shot when the opportunity presents itself," Liam says from behind me.

"You're right about that," Mikayla agrees. "TikTok is full of girls posting videos about how a lot of dudes out there aren't even trying. It's like they expect the woman to do the chasing. And then they wonder why they're still single. It makes the ones who try look good in comparison."

I add, "You'll always fail at something when you never try. It's also hard to miss Liam in a room, even when he tries to tell you that he's someone else. Didn't fool me for a second."

"Unfortunately, there are girls out there who probably believed him when he tried that on them before," Mikayla says with a shake of her head. "Okay, so when did you two know?"

"Know what?" I ask, unsure of what she means.

"Know that you wanted to get married," she clarifies.

Liam answers before I can formulate a believable response that doesn't include his bank account balance. "The first moment I saw her. Love at first sight." Oh, that's a good one.

Those who have experienced it will know exactly what he means, and those who haven't will take his word for it.

They both look at me in anticipation of my response. "For me, it was the moment that he asked me to marry him. I couldn't imagine saying anything but 'yes.' I didn't need time to think about it." It wasn't a lie; saying yes to Liam or someone similar to him was always a no-brainer for me. I'm relieved her question was specifically about knowing I wanted to marry him and not about knowing when I was in love with him. Those are two very different answers.

"That worked out well for you two then," Mikayla says and smiles. "It can be frustrating for the girl when she knows well before he catches on. I swear, I hinted for months that I wanted to get married, but Demetrius wanted to wait until he had a signed contract as a professional football player before he would propose."

"At least he didn't make you wait until he had a football championship ring like Arthur did," Liam says loud enough for his best friend to hear.

Arthur walks over to join our conversation. "Jen and I had been together long enough that I knew she was in it for the long haul."

"Bro, if you were that certain, you should have married her sooner," Liam argues. "Some people think that marriage is outdated, but there are still legal benefits to being married including insurance and tax benefits. Plus, it says a lot when you're willing to make a commitment that confirms you want to share everything including last names. Not that people have to change their names, but it is a statement."

I was still waiting for the official marriage certificate to come to do that very thing. Even if my marriage to Liam implodes in a few months, a possibility that seems less and less probable, it's beneficial to keep his last name. My mother's last name bears no significance or ties to it, but Liam's is recognizable in some circles of influence. It may even have more pull in the sports world than the last name of my

biological father. In America, football fans outnumber basketball fans.

"What matters is that they're married now," I say in
defense of Arthur. "If they had gotten married right out of
college, they might not have been able to afford the fancy
wedding that she got to have by waiting a few years."

"At least I invited my friends to my wedding," Arthur
points out to Liam. "Someone got married without telling the
rest of us until afterward."

Liam looks to me for help, but I shrug. "You would have
married her right then and there too if you were in my
shoes," he mumbles. "Life is too short to wait around for the
perfect moment."

Before any of us can respond, one of the other guys
gathers the team together for a game of flag football on the
lawn. Liam opens the pool shed and pulls out a plastic
container with the flags. None of the wives show concern that
one of them could get injured playing in the yard. Helen sits
in the empty chair next to me and Mikayla.

"They'll be fine as long as none of them escalate the game
to tackling," Helen says to reassure me. "Flag football is much
safer than what they do in Camelot Stadium or at practices.
It's how Liam started in football."

She was right. It was like watching their practice as they
ran plays and tried ridiculous distractions. Coach Anderson
stood on the sidelines and observed the men who were like
sons to him. I hadn't just married into money; I had married
into a gang of gladiators.

RULE #5

Pleasing his mother is the golden ticket to all things opulent

PRESEASON GAMES ARE important to the teams because it's when rookies and new players can prove themselves to either the team that initially signed them or another team that could sign them in the future. The Knights are one of the teams that everyone keeps their eyes on. Liam has always been a good tight end, but when Arthur became the starting quarterback, the symbiosis contributed to creating a championship team. One would still be good without the other, but together, they win championships.

Helen, the ultimate mom and assistant combo, treats preseason games as if they were the regular season even though her son won't play for more than the first quarter. Of the three preseason games on the schedule, only the first one is at home in Kansas City.

"You don't need to come to the road preseason games," Liam insists when I ask for the umpteenth time. "Sometimes coach doesn't even let me stay in the whole first quarter before he throws the second string guys in. It wouldn't be worth the time off work for you. Save that for the regular season."

Helen has learned the ins and outs of Camelot Stadium. Liam's whole professional career to this point has been in

Kansas City. With the big contract they gave Arthur to keep him here for the foreseeable future, Liam is likely to retire here. He's made it clear to the media that he cares more about winning than he does his individual stats and notoriety. The teams that build dynasties include top-tier players who are willing to get paid less than they would on another team to be the best together. Legends are rarely those who had the largest contract.

On game day, Liam leaves early to head to the stadium. Not long after he pulls out of the garage, Helen arrives with baked treats in tow and wearing a Knights jersey with Liam's number on it.

"Helen, just because Mudpie is a vegan bakery doesn't mean that it's healthy," I argue as I bite into one of the home-made blueberry pop tarts. I'm going to need to use the home gym after the game to make sure I burn off all this sugar.

"It's healthier than the premade breakfast items at the store," she argues, and I don't have a rebuttal for that. "I should get to spoil my kids whenever I please, even if they try to eat healthy."

I limit myself to one pop tart before making myself eggs and whole wheat toast to wash down the sugar. Helen makes herself at home, checking the items in the fridge and pantry to make a grocery list. She prefers going to the grocery store on Mondays when the majority of people are at work.

"What time do we need to leave?" I ask her before retreating to my bathroom to get ready.

"In half an hour," she says. "Even though we're not going through the parking and gates for general admission, it still takes time to park and get to the suites. We'll want to be there early enough for some of the pregame hype." By hype, she means the national anthem, the Knight's chant, and the flyover by the US Air Force jets. Due to the quality of television cameras, viewing from home is easier for watching purposes, but attending a game at Camelot is worth what people pay for the experience. The same concept applies to other teams and other sporting events.

I rush back to my closet and pull on the bejeweled Liam Cartwright jersey I'd managed to hide from Liam. Natalie had helped me find a place that does custom orders like this. I bought one in both his home and away jerseys. Seeing the sparkle from the diamond on my finger, I debate whether I want to wear the flashy ring to the game today. Taking it off will only delay the inevitable since the news of our marriage will come out one way or another. Now that everyone close to us knows, it's up to me to decide when I'll be comfortable facing the public's scrutiny. I keep the ring on. I've never cared much what people thought of me before, and I won't start now. I skip the heels and slip on sneakers instead since attending events at Camelot involves a lot of walking.

Satisfied with my appearance, I embark on the task of tracking down Helen in this giant house. I have yet to see anyone come here to clean the house, but the floors are never dusty. The magic must happen while I'm at work. Liam hires a company to clean since he has the money and incentive not to do it himself. For a man who plays a yard game professionally, he does not like his space dirty.

Helen is in the living room, looking out at the glittering reflection of the saltwater pool. It would be the perfect spot for a girls' day with Helen and Natalie if I can convince Liam to go hang out at Arthur's. Maybe Arthur's wife Jen would be up for joining us if I ever get the chance to meet her. She and the kids were sick on the day Liam had the team over to our house to introduce them to me.

"Do you want kids?" Helen asks me without breaking her focus on the backyard.

"I've never really thought about it," I answer truthfully. I'd been so focused on the husband and money part that I never considered life beyond getting what I wanted. "My mom hadn't planned on having me, but she knew she wanted me as soon as she found out she was pregnant. I guess I've always assumed that when and if that happens, I'll embrace it. And if I'm going to have one, I may as well have a few more so that they have each other. That's one thing I never had growing up that I wonder about sometimes."

Helen turns to look at me with a knowing smile. "Sometimes I wish I'd tried again to see if the third one was a girl, but keeping up with two boys was exhausting. Once I gave up on that dream, I started looking forward to the day that one of them would give me a daughter." Warmth spreads through me at the thought that I'm a dream come true for her. It almost outweighs the pang of guilt I feel for what started this.

"I'm ready to go when you are," I say to change the subject. I follow her to the garage and climb into the passenger side of her EV. One of the cons to electric vehicles is that they don't roar to life the way combustion engines do. Based on sound alone, you can't tell if the car is on.

Helen knows the fastest way from Liam's house to Camelot Stadium. The drive is about twenty minutes, but traffic patterns coming off the highway can be unpredictable on game days. Natalie isn't the biggest fan of football, but we attended one of the playoff games last season. Her family had access to a private suite that sheltered us from the frigid cold of the outside temperatures. The fans who pay extra to freeze during a playoff game are nothing short of dedicated.

The parking attendant recognizes Helen right away and gives us the VIP treatment. Being part of a player's family means special parking and exclusive entrances away from the crowds pouring into the stadium from the main gates. I stay close to my mother-in-law as she navigates us through security and all the nooks and crannies until we're in Liam's private suite. Through the glass, I see the red spots of Knights jerseys as fans trickle into their sections to find their seats. There aren't nearly as many fans of the opposing team in the audience, but that's to be expected for preseason matches.

Some teams won't play their starting quarterbacks at all until the regular season.

Liam's suite isn't as large as Arthur's, but it's more than enough space for me and Helen. If I had thought about it, I would have invited Natalie and a few of our friends to join me. The suite comes with complimentary food and drinks in addition to the air conditioning. This is how the wealthy enjoy the best of American sports. I'm grateful that Helen likes me enough to want to share Liam's suite with me and show me the ropes.

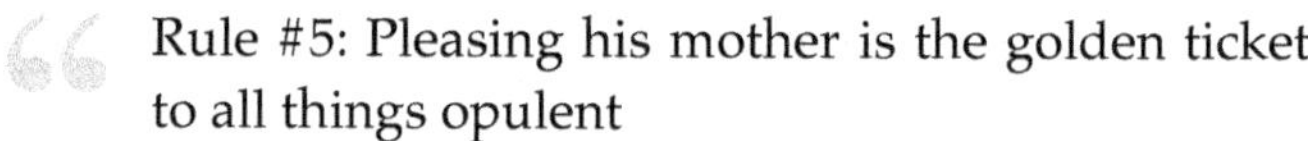

Rule #5: Pleasing his mother is the golden ticket to all things opulent

When the teams run onto the field from the tunnels, Liam looks up in our direction. His smirk is displayed on the large screens for all in attendance to see. Local channels are probably broadcasting his face to every single girl who might be watching.

Sasha joins us in the suite, taking the open seat to my left. When I glance over to her, she has social media open for any mentions of Liam. We were likely safe since preseason games aren't widely watched, but her job is to be prepared for any scenario. Arriving and sitting with Helen while wearing Liam's last name across my back could arouse suspicion from any of the security workers. The screens in the stadium don't show the same crowd shots as the ones viewers at home see, so it's hard to know if they'll show Helen cheering on her son in this particular game.

From the suite, I can see the mascot in a plush suit of armor and plastic sword as he walks through the aisles to take photos with fans. Our team wins the coin toss and chooses to defer and kick the ball to the other team. Our defense stops the other team from making it far down the field. After a few failed plays, their punt team runs onto the field as our receiving team waits for the football at the other end. After the receiver is tackled near the 20-yard line, I watch Arthur, Liam, and the Knights' starting offense run onto the field.

Play after play, the Knights move the ball closer to the red zone. Between crucial plays, they display their infamous "round table huddle." Then with a perfectly thrown pass from Arthur, Liam catches the ball in the end zone. He performs a touchdown dance that'll be turned into a GIF later. After the first offensive drive, Liam is on the sidelines for the remainder of the game. He and Arthur are side-by-side, discussing plays by the looks of it.

"Looks like we're in the clear for now," Sasha says while scrolling through her phone. "None of the cameras showed the suite, so no one has paid any attention to Odette. The first regular season home game will be a different story. It's a prime-time slot, and they love to show Helen."

"My son got his looks and TV personality from me," Helen says unashamedly. It's a wonder she hasn't starred in any ads with Liam yet. It would be a great way to show his family-friendly side.

We watch the remainder of the game while commenting on which players we guess will survive the first round of roster cuts in a few days. It's bittersweet to think that for some of them, their dream will end soon. A few will be signed to the practice squad where they might be elevated to the active roster if injuries prove it necessary. Others will be released back into the sea of professional football players who could be signed by another team's active roster or practice squad.

When the Knights secure their victory, Helen and Sasha walk me through their post-game ritual. Liam is often featured in post-game press conferences, but he opted out of that opportunity today to be able to leave with me sooner. On our way to see him, we run into Arthur's wife Jen with their two kids.

"Helen, it's nice to see you," she says as she hugs my mother-in-law. "Isn't it great to be back at Camelot again?"

"Your kids have grown so much since I last saw them," Helen says and smiles. She kneels to greet Arthur's five-year-old son.

"Hi, I'm Jen," she says and holds out her free hand that isn't holding her one-year-old daughter.

I shake her hand and say, "I'm Odette."

Recognition sparks in her eyes at hearing my name. "Odette, of course. That makes a lot of sense why you're here with Helen. I'm so sorry that we couldn't make it to your cookout. The stomach bug is no joke for adults, and it's ten times worse when both kids get it at the same time. It's a miracle Arthur managed not to catch it."

"I completely understand," I reassure her with a smile. "I'm glad you stayed home and rested. I don't think any of the players would have been happy if they caught it from you guys. They might be tough when tackling each other on the field, but I suspect some of them are babies when they're sick."

Jen laughs and says, "Arthur is a baby if he gets sick during the off-season. If it's during football season, he'll push through it even when he shouldn't. It's really about priorities for them."

Large hands snake around my waist from behind as I feel Liam's lips brush my cheek. "I like how you look in my last name," he says loud enough for anyone nearby to hear.

"Oh, that reminds me," Jen says. Without asking first, she grabs my left hand to inspect the ring Liam gave me. Arthur joins our group as the center diamond sparkles from the overhead light. "That's a nice ring, Liam. You get points for that one even though you didn't invite us to the wedding."

"They practically eloped," Arthur says as if that makes it any better. "We just have to convince them to have an official wedding." Sounds like everyone is in on this idea.

Liam pulls me close as he says, "I might be pushing my luck trying to get her to marry me more than once."

Our conversation is interrupted by one of the coaching staff grabbing Arthur for the press conference. Jen's daughter cries when her father walks away, which causes Jen to excuse herself. After a quick conversation with Liam, Helen dismisses herself, leaving me alone with my husband for the first time today.

"Do you want to eat out, or do you want to order pick-up?" Liam asks as he lets go of my waist to hold my hand.

"If we go out to eat, we're more likely to be spotted by someone who will recognize you," I point out as he leads me toward the VIP lot where his car is parked.

"We're still under the radar? I wasn't sure if they would give my suite much air time today."

"It's preseason. It's considered practice runs as far as the media is concerned. When the news breaks, will it be a good idea for us to go out after a game?"

Seconds of silence pass before Liam answers. "If we were just dating, I wouldn't care as much about the public image. I don't think it makes a difference either way since we're married though. I don't know if people will pay much attention to me tonight since the season isn't in full swing yet."

"Let's just get it for pick-up," I decide once we're in his car. "I didn't get a chance to work out before the game. Going out takes up more time than eating at home."

I WASN'T PREPARED for how empty the house would feel when Liam left town for his road games. It makes sense that Jen goes to all but the international games, and she has two kids to tote around with her. Taking the kids with you is just part of navigating the football world. Helen isn't even here to watch the game with me because she went with Liam as both his mom and assistant.

When I invite Natalie over to watch the game, I don't expect a response. She's glued to her phone at all times except when I need a quick response from her. This time though, she texts to say she's on her way with food. I switch the TV in the home theater to the channel with the broadcasting rights for the Knights' preseason games. I mute the volume when my phone buzzes with an incoming call from Natalie.

"Can you preheat the oven to 400 degrees?" She asks, but she doesn't wait for me to respond. "You caught me at the perfect time. I was just about to put this in the oven, but now I'll just use yours instead."

"I'll go do that right now," I say as I get up to head to the kitchen. "I should have invited you as soon as I knew I'd be staying in town. There's another one next weekend if you want to plan for that as well. To be honest, they're kind of boring since the wins and losses of the preseason don't affect the playoffs."

"You wouldn't feel that way if you were married to one of the backups instead of a starter," she says. "We'll talk when I get there. Bye!"

Five minutes later, she's at my front door with a glass dish in her hands. Whatever she made, it's covered with shredded cheese that'll melt in the oven. She follows me to the kitchen, places the food in the oven, and sets a timer.

"I need a bathroom, and then I expect a full tour of this house," she says in a way that makes me realize how much I miss her. For years, we lived together and saw each other every day. Strangely, this is the first time I've seen her in weeks.

I follow her demands as I take her on the same route Liam had when he showed me around my new home. Fortunately, I finally finished arranging my wardrobe this morning. Everything is neat and in its place. Natalie's family's home is still large compared to this one, but she shows an appreciation for the modern style and design of the backyard area.

"Liam must be doing well for himself even though he's

not getting paid as much as he could," Natalie says as she scopes out the basement gaming layout.

"He cares more about the legacy than the playing money," I say in his defense. "It's the smarter move in the long run. Being a big personality on a championship team opens doors for more endorsements and notoriety that will last beyond his years on the field. It's the best strategy for financial longevity. Plus, he's been smart with his investments."

"Oh, I'm aware," she says with a wink. "He's already approached the Knights ownership group about wanting to join them when he retires. Do you know what this house is missing? Photos on the wall. Nothing about this house makes it obvious who lives here. Most people have family photos to personalize the space."

"So I'm supposed to put up wedding pictures?" I ask sarcastically.

She thinks about my statement for a moment before she says, "You could still have a ceremony and reception with all of the normal stuff. Just tell people that you didn't want to wait until the offseason to be married, however, you want all the pomp and circumstance of a wedding. Buy a white dress, book a venue, and then go on a honeymoon. As happy as I am for you, I feel like I missed out on a big life event of yours. Your mom and his family likely feel the same way. It's up to you, though."

"I'll talk to Liam about it when he gets home," I say, already knowing he'll be in full support of the plan. So far, none of our friends and family have been upset about the news; they're more upset about not being a part of the moment. "It would be nice to have some photos up on the walls."

Arthur and Liam both start the game, but after their game-opening touchdown, Coach Wes pulls them from the field to give the backups more playing time. By then, the enchiladas that Natalie made are baked to perfection, and we eat while discussing possible venues if I were to have a wedding.

Kansas City has its fair share of beautiful backdrops, but with Liam's money, a destination wedding is an option. At the end of the day though, it'll be his decision on how much we spend. I might have married him for his money, but that doesn't mean I feel comfortable spending exorbitantly without his consent.

"What is Arthur's wife Jen like in person?" Natalie asks me as we clean up our plates. "Some people think she's stuck-up, but I've also heard the opposite. Sometimes a person can come off different from how they usually are depending on the context."

"I've only met her once, but she seems nice to me," I say with a shrug. "I think she's in a tough position because people who don't know her put labels on her that are far from the truth. For instance, there are women out there who will tear her down and call her a gold digger, but she was with Arthur for years before he became a professional athlete. She was a professional athlete herself before she decided that she would rather support him than play overseas. People need to stop making assumptions about her without knowing the whole story."

Natalie nods and says, "I agree. I can't tell you how many times I've had people assume I'm stuck up because of my family's wealth. Just because I have money doesn't mean I live with my head in the clouds."

"There are both rich and poor people who live with their heads in the clouds from being high on drugs," I say, remembering my cousin in Seattle. Fortunately, the last stint at rehab worked, and he's stayed clean for the last five years. The last thing I need is family members coming out of the woodwork for their piece of Liam's hard-earned money.

"What time is Liam supposed to be home?" Natalie asks and eyes the clock on the stove. "I want to make sure I'm out of here when he gets home so he can go straight to bed." Then, she winks at me. I roll my eyes at her insinuation.

"They're in Seattle, so it's about a three to three-and-a-half hour flight. It'll take them an hour or two for the post-game press conferences and clearing out the stadium. I don't expect him to be home until nine or later tonight, so we still have a few hours."

Natalie looks like she's ready to throw a full-fledged slumber party like she used to in boarding school. "Well, I'm going to leave the enchiladas here for him or for you to have later. I'll get the glass pan back from you when I come over for next week's game. We're going to have a girls' night, minus a few hours. My only question is this—Mamma Mia! or High School Musical?"

RULE #6

Proving yourself may require fighting fire with fire

THE CITY IS electric with the anticipation of the season's home opener at Camelot Stadium. There are events all week throughout the metro including the official Red Friday. During football season in Kansas City, people wear their Knights shirts and jerseys the Friday before a game to show collective support for the hometown team. This particular game is during the Thursday night prime-time slot, which results in Red Wednesday. The diehard fans wear their gear all week.

In addition to practices, Liam attends a handful of events including one for the charity he started. We only see each other early in the morning before we leave and late at night when we're too exhausted to do anything but fall asleep in the same bed. I silently wonder if it'll be like this the whole season, but I know it's likely an exception since it's the start. I'm working a half day on Thursday and taking Friday off since we won't get home from the game until after midnight.

When I wake up Thursday morning to the sound of clanging in the kitchen, I expect to find my mother-in-law at the stove. I round the corner to find Jeff the Chef expertly chopping and dicing vegetables for the protein breakfast scramble he's cooking for me and Liam.

"How soon will breakfast be ready?" I ask him as I drink a glass of water.

"Might be another thirty minutes," he says without smiling. Jeff rarely smiles from what I've seen of him so far. "You have time to go do a workout." Liam must have clued him into the routine I've started. On the mornings that I don't meet Gabe at the gym close to work, I've been doing my workouts in the gym here at the house. Gabe is still begging for a chance to meet my new husband, but Liam's schedule has been too crazy to join me.

I quickly change into my tank top and yoga pants and decide on an indoor cycling workout. I have yet to see Liam use any of the high-end equipment in his house, but I'm sure he makes use of it during the off-season. He comes to let me know that breakfast is ready when I have about three minutes left in the workout. I finish and do a quick cool down before joining him at the kitchen island. More times than not, we eat here rather than at the formal dining room table. Jeff has already disappeared, leaving us alone for this brief bubble of time.

"On a scale of one to ten, how excited are you for tonight?" I ask him to gauge how awake he is.

"Eleven," he teases. "Normally it's a ten for the season opener, but I have a pretty plus-one coming to watch me tonight. I'm trying to impress her so that she keeps coming to my games. It's the dream to get to play my favorite game well in front of my favorite girl."

"Liam, you know your mom will still love you even if you fumble the ball," I tease back.

He steals a bite of my omelet even though his serving is the same. "Oh, I know my mom will be there. It's my wife that I'm trying to win over. She hasn't even agreed to go to Europe to see me play."

"Hey, I told you to let me know if the schedule for that week is even worth my going with you. I don't want to fly all that way to spend our time there jet-lagged at the hotel or the stadium. If you're flying the Thursday before the game, you'll only be there two full days."

He concedes. "I know, I know. I'm still waiting for Coach to give me an answer. They're working out the details for the chartered plane. I'd rather spend weeks with you in Europe solely as a vacation. Frankfurt will be a work trip more than anything else given how hard the league is promoting over there. I heard the tickets sold out within ten minutes of going live for sale, and it's mostly Europeans who bought the seats."

"Either way, I'll go if you want me there," I promise. "I need to finish getting ready for work. I'll see you before the game on the field?"

"I'm going to kiss you in front of everyone." It's a threat to what little privacy we still have, but I don't doubt his follow-through.

THE PRESEASON GAME was a warmup compared to the crowds gathered at Camelot Stadium today. News stations report that lines were forming as early as sunrise even though the gates don't open until four and a half hours before kickoff. With kickoff scheduled for 7:30 in the evening, some fans will be waiting nearly half the day just to be the first to enter the parking lot. From what I've heard, tailgating at Camelot is its own unique experience and the best in the league.

At lunchtime, I drive home to eat lunch with Helen. Daniel Cartwright's flight is due to land at the airport any minute now, and his guest room is ready for his arrival. Whether or not Helen is ready for his arrival is another story entirely.

"When was the last time you saw him?" I ask her before taking a bite of my Greek salad.

"At the league championship game," she says without

hesitation. That is a fairly memorable time, though. Liam won his second league championship that night, and both his parents and his brother had been there to congratulate him. Because football season encompasses both Thanksgiving and Christmas, that championship was one of the few times in the year their whole family was together to celebrate.

"Wouldn't it be crazy if they won two years in a row?" I say thinking back on when the Knights won for the first time in fifty years. All the football fans in the region were ready to crown Arthur as their sports king after the late comeback in that game. That whole playoff run consisted of the Knights coming back and winning after being down more than one score. Winning set the bar and expectations high for the Knights franchise. The following year, they lost the league championship in a match that was painful to watch due to the numerous injuries and penalties on the Knights. Last year, Arthur led the team to another victorious ending. It was only a matter of time before the team earned another.

Helen looks thoughtful as she says, "After last year, I don't think the sports commentators are underestimating the Knights anymore. It was supposed to be a rebuilding season to train up the rookies and young players. The Knights recruiting office is proving to be one of the best as of late. I mean, they drafted my son, so someone there knows what they're doing."

I smile at her comment. She would be proud of him even if he had tanked once in the league. Some players peak in college, but others reach their potential with the right coaching and team environment. The Knights put the time and energy into both after years of problems.

I'm not the only Cartwright wearing a bejeweled jersey today. Helen ordered herself one after seeing mine at the preseason game. I touch up my hair and makeup knowing that the cameras are more likely to show Liam's suite tonight. Tonight is a prime-time game featuring the defending champions. Millions of eyes will be watching across the nation and possibly in others around the world. My mother, who has never had an interest in football, is planning to tune in to see Liam play. It's a high-stakes night, and Sasha and Natalie are both meeting us at the stadium.

"Do I look like I could be married to a football player?" I ask Helen as we head to the garage to leave.

"You look like Liam Cartwright's perfect match," she says in response. Her approval should be enough. I'm usually confident and secure in my own skin, but something about this game has me on edge. Liam's promise from this morning plays on repeat in my head, both dreading and anticipating the reactions from potential onlookers. For someone who wants to let the media and public make their own theories about our romance, he doesn't seem to want to see how long he can hide me.

An incoming phone call from Daniel Cartwright flashes across the infotainment touchscreen in Helen's car. I've been so caught up on the media noticing me tonight that I forgot I'll also be meeting Liam's dad for the first time.

Helen answers the call. "Hey, Dan. I'm in the car with Odette on the way to the stadium. Are you on your way there?"

"I just got in my Uber. The new airport terminal is a big upgrade compared to the old ones," his voice says over the car's sound system. "For a minute, I thought I had landed in the wrong city until I remembered all the news stories about this project."

"I forgot that it wasn't open yet at the end of last season," Helen says in response to her husband. It must be strange to go months without seeing the man you're still married to. I pray that the suite isn't awkward with the two of them present. Liam would warn me if he suspected things might be strained between his parents, more than the existing strain from his father's stubbornness about moving to Kansas City.

Even with the recycled air turned on, I can smell the

smoke from the tailgate. Rows upon rows of cars with lawn chairs and grills fill the parking lot as fans eat and play games on the asphalt. Barbecue is one of Kansas City's specialties, but the season ticket holders have been known to get creative with the food they serve at their tailgate parties. One of the downsides to being a player on the field is that Liam doesn't get to experience this side of the fandom. He's one of many that they're all here to see.

The Truman Sports complex houses both Camelot Stadium and the soon-to-be-obsolete baseball stadium. The major league team that's been next door to the Knights since the sports complex opened in the 1970s is working on a deal to build a downtown stadium. Whether they move to one of the downtown neighborhoods or north of the river, the Knights will be the only team here in the future.

"Can you imagine how crazy the traffic will be when the largest international soccer tournament is here?" I say to Helen as we walk into the stadium.

"That could depend on whether the games hosted in Kansas City attract more Americans or more of the international crowd," Helen says thoughtfully. "Americans are used to being dependent on their cars except for those who live downtown or in places with efficient public transportation like New York City. International travelers are more likely to be open to taking the bus options that they'll have specifically for the matches. It's a shame that the east-west streetcar project won't be a reality until after the soccer tournament, although I heard it won't be going as far east as the stadiums."

"I used the streetcar to get to work when I lived downtown," I tell Helen as we go through security. "Even in winter, it wasn't too bad unless there was snow and ice."

Sasha appears seemingly out of nowhere as she directs us toward the entrance to the field level. "Any sign of Dan yet?" Helen asks her.

"Security is supposed to notify me when he gets here,"

Sasha replies. The publicist is on her phone as she walks, but I assume she knows where we're going. This is part of her routine after years in the business. "Liam should be waiting at this end of the field." We follow the light as we walk out of the shadows and into the disappearing sunlight. By the time the game begins, the sun will be sinking below the horizon.

I know which one is my husband as soon as my eyes adjust to the brightness of the field. He jogs toward us with his helmet in his hands and his smile as bright as the stadium lights at night. A few yards down from us, Arthur is holding his daughter while talking to Jen. If I hadn't seen their kids with my own eyes, I would question how she could look that fit in her red leather pants after giving birth to two children. Keeping a consistent workout routine and diet during pregnancy worked in her favor.

I'm entirely unprepared despite the warning bells. When he's a few feet away, Liam drops his helmet on the grass to free his hands. I expect a hug when he pulls me close, but instead, he lifts me off my feet and kisses me like he said he would. If there are news cameras around, I don't notice. I'm dialed into the way he smiles against my lips and the cheers coming from his teammates.

"That had better be on your list of top ten kisses," he says as he sets me down.

"Am I supposed to be keeping track of your performances?" I ask and wipe my lip gloss off his mouth with my thumb. "If so, I might need an instant replay of that one later."

"Liam, your dad just arrived. Do you have enough time for him to come join us here, or should I have security escort him to your suite?" Sasha interrupts the moment. She has her phone to one ear on a call, the other person waiting for her instructions.

Liam checks the time on my watch and calculates, "Go ahead and bring him out here. I want to be the one to introduce him to Odette." I release a breath I didn't know I was holding. Knowing Liam will be present for the first impression eases my nerves.

Sasha steps away to relay Liam's decision while Helen steps closer to pull her oldest son into a hug. "You're wearing matching jerseys with my name on them," he states the obvious. "Can I get one too, or do they not offer them in my size? I want to be able to tell people that I'm your Knight in shining armor."

"Odette, I apologize for my son's sense of humor," Helen says. "I can assure you that he doesn't get it from me."

"It's from my side," a familiar voice says from a man who looks like an older version of Liam. Liam is a few inches taller and bulkier than his dad, but the resemblance is uncanny. "That's why they're called 'dad jokes.'"

Liam and I both catch the way his parents look at each other. I'm not one for committing crimes, but I'll dabble in arson if it means Dan has to move here out of necessity. I would hate for Liam's childhood home to burn down as collateral damage in the parent trap. It's a small price to pay to reunite true love, though.

Liam wraps his dad in a hug before introducing me to him. "Dad, this is my wife Odette. Odette, this is my dad, Daniel Cartwright."

I shake Daniel's outstretched hand, unsure if this is normal. Who am I kidding? Nothing about this situation is normal. Most fathers don't meet their new daughter-in-law for the first time on the sidelines of a football field mere hours before the opening game of the professional league season. It's even stranger for me because I grew up without a father or any father figure in my life. Dan is now the closest thing I have to that.

Arthur calls Liam over to go to the locker room and do the final preparations before their grand entrance later. Liam kisses me one more time and runs off to join his teammates, picking up his helmet along the way. Sasha ushers us off the field and to Liam's suite. Natalie is perched on a chair when we arrive.

"I can't believe it's taken me this long to come to a game since moving back to Kansas City," she says as she turns to look out at the field. "Camelot Stadium is still one of the best in the league in terms of in-person experience. It's why superstars like Beyoncé and Taylor Swift included this stadium on their tours."

"You forgot to add Ed Sheeran to that list," I say and pull her into a hug. "Thanks for slumming it down here with us instead of in the owner's suite."

Natalie turns to Helen and says, "Oh, please, getting to watch the game with Helen Cartwright is far from slumming it. It's much more interesting here than it is where all the owners do is talk business."

"Dan, this is Odette's best friend, Natalie Cornwall," Helen says to her husband, and his eyes light up with recognition. Dan isn't even from Kansas City, but he knows who the Cornwalls are and their significance for both the city and the team. "She's the mastermind who orchestrated the night Liam and Odette met." Natalie might have been the one to bring me to the club where Liam was, but I was the one who masterminded my way into his life for the foreseeable future. He simply made it easier to do than I had assumed it would be.

Although a wall of windows separates us from the rest of the crowd, we can feel the energy when the fans enter the stadium. I'm thankful for the suite with its amenities, but part of me wishes I could be among the masses as they chant and echo throughout the modern-day coliseum.

"What are some of your favorite stadiums that you've been to when watching Liam's games?" I ask both Helen and Dan.

"That fancy new stadium in LA is very nice," Dan says as his wife thinks through the plethora of games she's traveled to. "Since it's an indoor stadium, the screens are in the middle of the field, which makes it easier to see."

Natalie comments, "You would think that somewhere with more moderate weather like LA wouldn't need an indoor stadium as much as some other places."

"LA is where the money is at," Helen and Dan say at the same time. Is this what they're like all the time? Next, they'll be finishing each other's sentences. Apart from the years that we lived near my grandparents, I'd never experienced a normal family dynamic. Not that Helen and Daniel's long-term separation is normal by any means. Natalie's parents are still married and in love, but we didn't spend much time with them during our short stint in their guest house.

"San Francisco has a cool stadium," Helen says to bring us back to my question. "They have gardens at the stadium that grow food used by the concessions. I'm not a big fan of San Francisco the city, but that's a great way to use fresh ingredients. When Liam retires, I might have enough time to finally start a garden."

Dan laughs and says, "When that boy retires from football, it'll be to pursue the next thing he's passionate about. You might be just as busy helping him with the next project or with any future grandchildren." Dan winks at me with that last statement.

With how fast and busy life has been, Liam and I haven't even talked about whether either of us wants kids. Kids add a new level of complication. Kids tie two people together for life whether they make their marriage work or not except in the case of my absent father. I'm just trying to learn the ropes of life in the professional football world.

Out on the field and displayed on the two large screens at the ends of the field, we watch the players as they run out of the tunnel and onto the grass. Kansas City's team plays on a natural grass field, among the best in the league. We hear the roar of the crowd as it rumbles through the stadium. The Knights' fans boo when the opposing team, the Barracudas, runs onto the field. Camelot Stadium holds the record for the loudest outdoor stadium in the world, and it wouldn't surprise me if they reach close to the record regularly. This fan base is loud. Playing at home gives the Knights an advantage because they're acclimated to the volume. Other teams have been known to practice in loud environments specifically to prepare themselves for the crowd at Camelot Stadium.

I turn around to check on Sasha who is scrolling and refreshing the social media feeds. A new commercial starring Liam is scheduled to air tonight during the second quarter. I don't know the details about his endorsements, but I know he has a few pending deals that could open doors in the future. As if she can feel my stare, she looks up from her phone.

"You're out there," she says calmly. "It's just one photo, and there's not much traction on it yet, but someone posted a picture of that on-field kiss. The angle doesn't show the ring, so it's still not completely out."

Of course, someone was around to snap a photo of the kiss. I move to sit in the chair beside her to see the photo for myself. Wow, we look cute. These jeans certainly do look as good as they feel. Within seconds, both Natalie and Helen are also inspecting the photo and the caption with the post. "Liam's new catch" as if I'm a football or a fish. Very original.

"You're all missing the flyover jets," Dan says as he looks out the glass. We may not be able to see them, but we can certainly hear them.

"Send me that link," Natalie says to Sasha before we return our attention to the game about to kick off. The Knights win the coin toss and opt to receive the ball in the second half. During the last few seasons, the Knights gained a reputation for having an offense that was significantly better than their defense and special teams in the rankings. The rankings are misleading though because the Knights' place-kicker and punter are two of the best in the league. As expected, the ball flies into the end zone.

Here's where I'm glad Liam is out on the field playing

instead of watching the game with me. Most guys see me and assume that I know very little about the sport. I don't know whether or not it's the default perception about girls in general or if I fit some stereotype in their heads. Either way, they tend to explain the basics to me while I pretend that I'm not annoyed. I was thorough in my research involving eligible bachelors in Kansas City, and being thorough includes knowing the mechanics of the major sports. Understand the sport, understand the man. I reserve showing my knowledge for situations when I want to impress. Liam has never tried to explain anything that I didn't first ask.

Helen and Dan are just as invested in the defense as they are when Liam and the rest of the starting offense are on the field. A large part of the rebuild includes drafting younger and faster players on the defense. Rookies put less financial strain on the team's salary cap and are eager to learn. Last year's draft class played a large part in the league champi-onship victory.

I'm on the edge of my seat when the defense sacks the Barracuda's quarterback on the third down. They punt the ball, which rolls out of bounds at the 18-yard line. Liam runs out onto the field with Arthur and the other Knights as they gather in their round table huddle. They've been working on a variation of their play known as Excalibur, but Liam didn't think they would have to wield that one in tonight's game. Coach Wes is known for his creative play calls as well as encouraging the team to come up with their own.

"That's my baby!" Helen stands and yells when Liam catches the ball and runs enough for the next first down. "He's showing off tonight."

"Let's hope for all our sakes that you're his new good luck charm," Daniel says to me as Liam makes another catch and runs for ten yards. My presence has nothing to do with how well he's playing. He and Arthur are in sync tonight, and it's evident on the field. The defense will adjust and double up on

Liam soon, but he'll dodge them and get himself open until they do. His best games look a lot like this one does.

When another receiver catches the touchdown pass, Liam joins in on the touchdown dance. We're jumping and cheering in the suite, and the extra kick is good. Those watching at home are seeing a commercial break, but at the stadium, the cameras are showing things like a kiss cam or other interactive displays to keep the fans engaged. Natalie is looking at the photo of me and Liam kissing on social media.

"The comments are already getting hateful," she warns me as she locks her phone screen.

I debate for a second before I ask her to show me. While the majority of comments are inquisitive and supportive, a few have left comments about how they think I look in my jeans or how no girl will be good enough for Liam. The negative comments must be from the same crowd that trolls Jen's social media accounts.

"Wow, I'm surprised at some of the creative insults they have about my butt as if having a big butt is a bad thing," I say with sarcasm as I hand her phone back.

"They're just jealous that you're the tight end they can see in that photo," she jokes, and Helen snorts.

Sasha looks up from her phone for a moment and says, "Odette, I'm going to post that photo of you and Liam tomorrow morning. It'll help silence some of the chatter online, but I don't want that to be the focus of the post-game conference. Tomorrow night, we're going to brainstorm ways to possibly sway some of the unfavorable responses. We may need to take an unconventional approach to this. Feed them spice instead of sugar."

"I'm fine with whatever you think is best," I say to her as the offense runs back on the field for another drive. "Liam is the one you'll have to convince."

"I may need your help with that one," she says with her attention returned to her phone screen. That can't be good for her eyes or her posture, but I'm no expert about either. I'm always hyper-aware of whether I'm slouching or hunched over though.

When the fourth quarter starts, it's a one-score game. The other team's defense has started double-teaming Liam, but he's honed in on what they're doing. Somehow, I know what he and Arthur are going to do next to mix things up. Liam dubbed this particular play "In the Stone." Seeing the moving parts in the context of a game is different from the Xs and Os he tried to draw on a piece of paper for me.

The play-call works well enough that Liam runs the ball into the end zone for the game-winning touchdown. He breaks out into dance moves similar to what I saw the first night at the club when we met. Although there's enough time remaining on the clock that the other team could potentially tie the game, our defense makes a stop that'll put them high in the rankings for this first week of the season.

By the time Liam stands up at the podium for the post-game conference, the internet has multiple articles about the new girl on his arm. It's shocking how fast some made the connection. In under an hour, I've gained thousands of followers who seem to be certain that I'm the girl who matches the back of the head of the girl in the photo. That and Liam previously liked nearly all of my photos posted from the last year per Sasha's suggestion.

"Liam, social media is blowing up with a photo of you and a special guest you had at the game," one reporter starts. "Can you tell us anything about her or how serious your relationship is?"

"I was beginning to think that the girl of my dreams didn't exist, but it's when I was ready to give up that I met her," he answers convincingly. "They always say that's when it happens, and I think they're right on the money."

"Excuse me," another reporter pipes up. "Who is 'they'?"

With a straight face, Liam says, "'They' is artificial intelligence." Whether they find the joke funny or not, all the reporters laugh at his comment. I need to find out who to complain to about the media encouraging my husband's bad jokes. It does the trick though because the questions that follow are all related to their win tonight and his outlook on the season ahead rather than his new relationship.

⬤

"I KNOW you said that you didn't want to make up a story to tell the media about your relationship, but I think we should at least be the ones to tell the world that the two of you are married," Sasha says to Liam as we eat the homemade pizza Helen made for us. She's here for moral support, but I also know she can talk sense into Liam if neither Sasha nor I can.

"What would that accomplish versus waiting?" He's not shutting down the idea, but he does want to know the logic behind her suggestion.

I open up my social media account to show him the comments on the photo of us posted this morning. It's a mixed bag of reactions, but the prominent theme among the comments is that I'm just another girl who will be in his past in a few weeks. It wasn't until the news came from one of us that I could see the real source of the negativity. While there are comments specifically criticizing me with irrelevant comparisons to his exes or the celebrities they think he should date, the source of doubt has nothing to do with me. Liam has been single for the last few years, but before that, he was notorious for being a playboy in the eyes of the media. These comments are questioning Liam's intentions for a serious relationship.

His face reveals a storm of emotions as he sees the internet's reaction to us—to him. "It's been years since I was that guy, but some people will never let me forget the mistakes of my past." I reach over to squeeze his hand in understanding.

"None of those people know the whole story," Helen says as she squeezes his other hand. "They've seen you on TV either on the field or in advertisements, but they don't know the work you've put into your own maturity and emotional stability. None of them know that you've already made the most serious commitment of all to her."

I can't say that it felt serious when I said yes to marrying him; it felt like finally achieving a lifetime goal, not making a lifetime promise. But I did make that promise to the one man who seemed the least likely to rush into something like this. Sasha sees the big picture, though. She was a big part of cleaning up his public image while he confronted his demons behind closed doors.

"I think we should stage some wedding photos and post them," Sasha drops the bomb. "We could even caption it with something like 'For those of you who think I'd never commit.' I don't think this is a situation where we should play nice because we've been playing nice for the last two years. I don't want to pull punches when it comes to this. You've worked too hard for people to continue to paint you as an immature frat boy."

> Rule #6: Proving yourself may require fighting fire with fire

"When do you think we could do the photo shoot?" Liam asks. "Between practices and games and Odette's regular day job, we only see each other at the beginning and end of the day."

Sasha looks as if a light bulb has just turned on in her head. "Odette, is what you do every day your dream job?"

"No," I say without hesitation. "Why?"

"You don't need to work a full-time job if you don't want to," she replies as if it were obvious. "You shouldn't spend so much of your time at a job that you aren't passionate about if you don't want to. In case you missed the memo, your husband makes millions of dollars each year. You have the flexibility to use your time differently."

I know she's right, but I don't want to admit the reason

why I didn't immediately quit after the wedding. Liam's face wordlessly says "See, I'm not the only one who thinks it's reasonable for you to put in your notice at work."

I sigh and say, "I'll think about it. I hate to leave the company in the lurch, so if I do leave my job, it'll be after I train my replacement."

"Liam, your wife is too good for you," Sasha says jokingly. "Helen, can you find some wedding dress shops near where Odette works so she can try some on during her lunch breaks this week? The sooner we can get this done, the better. Make sure they know it's for a high-profile client so that they don't try to give you an appointment weeks from now."

Helen beams at the prospect of shopping for wedding dresses. "Doesn't it take months to do fittings for wedding dresses?" I ask.

"Why won't we have an actual wedding instead of just staging one?" Liam asks before Sasha or Helen can answer mine. I hadn't brought up the idea to him yet since I didn't want to distract him from the season opener.

"Liam Cartwright, are you proposing to me?" I tease, but his eyes meet mine with the same serious intensity he had before the first time he kissed me.

With no regard for our audience, he pulls me into his lap and says, "I want a real wedding with you. I know I'm the one who rushed things when we got married, but I missed out on seeing you walk down the aisle in a white dress. Or any color dress, pantsuit, or outfit you prefer. We can do anything you want within reason."

If Sasha is annoyed that we derailed her publicity brainstorming session, she hides it well. "Let's pivot my original suggestion then. Instead of posting a wedding photo, we stage an elaborate proposal and share sneak peeks as you plan the wedding. It's not quite as shocking to the public as a surprise wedding, but it still shows a level of commitment from Liam that they're not used to seeing."

"Oh, this comment is a good one," I say after reading one

of the newer reactions to my photo. "This user said, 'The only commitment I care about is whether Liam is going to stay with the Knights until he retires. It's rare to find a talented player who's willing to play for the same team his whole career!'"

"At least someone gets it," Liam mutters. "Okay, I need to make sure Odette's name is added to my credit cards and bank account. Or, will it look suspicious if she's paying for things with the name Odette Cartwright?"

My brain is hitting the point in the night where I'm ready to shower and crawl into bed. I'm impressed at how quickly Liam recognized the snag before my mind had registered his words.

"I'll take care of it," Helen says. "You focus on football. I know you want to be involved in all the details, but you have plays to memorize and a game to be ready for. Your next game is on the road against a division opponent. I'll take care of planning with Sasha and Odette while you do what you need to do to win the next one. The last thing we need is people accusing Odette of being a distraction to you."

Sasha adds, "Ideally, we want you playing your best now that she's in the picture. The fans have tasted what it's like to attend two championship parades, and they're as eager for another win as you are. You have the opportunity to be the first back-to-back champions in almost twenty years."

"Should I leave off my wedding ring until we make the marriage official to the public?" Liam asks Sasha. Neither photo of us circulating the internet has a closeup of our hands to show the rings we exchanged. After weeks of getting used to mine, I would feel naked without it on.

Her expression says it all, and Liam slips the band off his left hand and gives it to me for safekeeping. I unclasp the gold chain from around my neck and string his ring through it before refastening the necklace. Anyone who notices it is likely to assume it's a family heirloom rather than the famous tight end's wedding ring. Under the bright lights of our living room, I can see a slight tan line from the rubber version he wears during practices. Since he normally wears gloves during games, none of the footage would reveal the band he's been wearing underneath. Liam stretches out his left hand as if he's trying to familiarize himself with the feeling of his bare ring finger.

"Oh, and before I forget," Sasha says as she walks toward the front door to leave, "Odette, we need you to go to the game in Germany."

RULE #7

Never refuse a Hampton vacation

Although I shouldn't and despite that this was my plan all along, I dread the conversation I need to have with my boss. This job might not be my passion, but it is something that I've invested time and energy to improve and grow in. The fact that I at least tried to continue working should ward off suspicions of my gold-digger tendencies.

When I ask Jack if I can talk to him when he's free, he says, "If you're giving me your two week's notice, then I need you to help train my niece to fill your position." I fail to hide the shock from my face because then he adds, "I'm surprised you stuck around as long as you did after getting married. I still want those tickets though if the offer stands."

"Of course, the offer still stands," I tell him, recovering from the unexpected turn in the conversation. All morning, I had been preparing myself to break the news to him, but he was already anticipating my announcement. "How soon is your niece starting?"

Jack looks at the time on his computer display and says, "Tomorrow morning if I can bribe her to come that soon. She'll go on spontaneous nights out and road trips with her friends, but when it comes to things like work, she claims she needs notice."

"I'll text my mother-in-law to remind her about those tickets," I say in response to Jack's rant about my successor.

When I leave my boss's office, I do just that. Within an hour, she sends the tickets Jack requested along with complimentary parking passes and VIP clearance. The woman knows how to pull strings and move mountains. She managed to get me an appointment under an alias at one of the most popular wedding dress boutiques in the city for the week following the team's bye week. According to the timeline that Sasha emailed us this morning, the proposal news will go live during the bye week following the game in Germany. There's a lot I'll be able to learn from both of them when I'm no longer working my full-time job.

While Sasha's timeline details the proposal and wedding-related social media posts, her email is devoid of locations apart from the days we'll be in Germany. The teams all have different rules for how they handle bye weeks, and the Knights give the players the week off. Now that I won't be working, Liam and I could theoretically go somewhere together that week. He might prefer to stay in town and use the extra prep and recovery time. The game after the bye week will be one of the most difficult opponents of the season.

As I sit in the rush hour traffic heading south from the downtown loop, it seems as if life is moving faster than the cars around me. Considering how slowly this section of the highway is, snails could accelerate faster. For once, I beat Liam home and preheat the oven for the dish prepped by Jeff the Chef. I think I got him to smile when I offered to bake the chicken if he seasoned it for us. He still refuses to tell me what he puts on his baked chicken, but he underestimates how stubborn and tenacious I am.

Before the oven has reached the optimal temperature, Liam walks in from the garage, his skin covered in a layer of sweat. It might be autumn according to the calendar, but the summer temperatures are holding on for as long as possible. Some days, it's warm enough that I wear sandals even as the leaves transform into brilliant reds, oranges, and yellows. Unlike me, part of Liam's days are outdoors in the heat that won't go away quite yet.

He looks as if he's going to head to the bathroom to shower when he pauses and turns toward me. "Arthur and Jen want to know if we would like to spend the bye week with them in the Hamptons. Think about it while I go shower," he says as if he were passing along an invitation to the neighborhood park. I've been to the Hamptons a few times with Natalie, but this is more than just an invitation to a popular vacation spot among the wealthy; this is a stamp of approval from Liam's best friend and his best friend's wife. These are the important people in his life setting out the welcome mat for me to be part of their world like he is.

Rule #7: Never refuse a Hampton vacation

There isn't anything to think over. They could have been inviting us to the jungles of Africa, and I would have said yes and scheduled my yellow fever vaccination. I have questions about the details, but that doesn't dampen my excitement for a vacation. When the oven beeps to notify me it's reached the selected temperature, I slide the glass dish filled with seasoned chicken breast onto the rack and set the timer per Jeff's instructions. I can follow instructions even though I might not be the best cook. I slide onto the barstool at the kitchen island and make a rough outline for training Jack's niece to take over my role at work.

I am so engrossed in my task that I smell Liam before I hear or see him. He wraps his arms around me from behind and kisses my cheek. One thing I didn't anticipate in all my scheming and planning is how easy it could be to be with and around someone. Being around him feels like being at home.

Seeing the timer on the stove, he pulls out a pan to boil water for brown rice to accompany the chicken. I have no problems cooking white kinds of rice such as jasmine and basmati, but brown rice never cooks correctly when I try. The only times I've gotten it right are when I used a rice cooker. Liam gets it perfect every time as if he has the kitchen equivalent of a green thumb. A golden spatula? When the timer has ten minutes remaining, I add the chopped veggies to the chicken.

"What are your thoughts about going on vacation with Arthur and Jen?" Liam asks once we sit down with our plates full of steaming food.

"Absolutely," I respond before taking my first bite. It's still too hot to eat without burning my tongue, but I chew and swallow before sipping my water. "I was hoping we could go somewhere during your break since I gave my two weeks' notice at work today."

Liam's face shifts to an excited expression at my news. It's a relief that he's happy I won't be working a full-time job. "You've been so busy between work and coming to my games, I was slightly concerned that you wouldn't have enough time to stop and think about what you might want to do instead of that job," he admits sheepishly. "It would have been fine through most of the season, but once I'm in the off-season, I'm going to want more time with you. It seemed that would be impossible if you were working a traditional 9-5 or 8-5 or whatever hours you're at the office."

"The commute from here to downtown certainly doesn't make it any shorter," I add. "It was a great job when I could take the streetcar from my apartment, but rush hour traffic gets old. The sad part is that Kansas City traffic is minimal compared to that of other cities. Here, it's just frustrating because it's unpredictable from day to day. The same drivers will go ten miles under the speed limit and then speed to ten over the limit less than five minutes later. You don't have to deal with it as much because on game days, you're getting there before the majority of people and leaving after the stadium has nearly emptied."

"If I'd known the commute was stressing you out that much, I would have called your boss and bribed him to fire you," he jokes, and I playfully hit his arm. Despite how light my jab is compared to the hits he takes during games, he winces. I lift the sleeve of his shirt to inspect his arm. His skin is purple and bruised in the spot where I had hit him.

I meet his eyes and ask, "Is that from the game, or is that from practice?"

"We were running a new play at practice today, and one of the running backs got a little turned around," he says as he shrugs off the minor injury. "It looks worse than it feels."

Despite his brushing it off, I kiss it like my mom used to when I would fall and hurt myself. It shouldn't feel this natural to want to take care of him. We're still in the early stages of our relationship in the grand scheme of things. He hasn't even met my mother yet.

"My mom has a break between movies coming up the first week of October," I say to him, remembering the text message she sent me earlier today. "She wants to come to Kansas City and get to know you a bit." What she really wants to do is scope out the multi-million-dollar house and the lifestyle of her new son-in-law. Whether she'll admit it to herself or not, I suspect part of her wants to see what her life could have been like had my biological father wanted to commit to her and stay part of our lives.

"What are the dates? My dad will be here for the home game that first weekend, but the second weekend is on the road. She can stay with my mom if she's here for the home game. She's welcome to come with us if it's the second weekend. My mom wants to meet her."

I don't think about it long before I ask, "Why doesn't your dad stay with your mom when he comes into town since they still seem to want to be together? They are legally married, after all, and neither of them is dating other people from what I've been able to gather."

Liam laughs and shakes his head before giving me a wry smile. "It's all part of their mutual agreement to never be left alone in a room together. Neither of them wants to be with anyone else, but they're also both too stubborn to let go and compromise on the reason they're separated. It's gone on so long now, but it has yet to change. My dad knows that if he stays with her, he'll never leave. He let her come here to help me, but he doesn't have it in him to leave her. And my mom likes it here too much to move back with him even though I could easily hire a different assistant."

"Helen is a huge part of your daily support system," I argue. "That's so much more than an assistant. I still don't understand why he won't move here."

"At first, he stayed there to help my grandfather who was having some health problems, but my grandfather passed away two years ago. Now, I think my dad is having a hard time letting go of the life we all had together. I would understand if my brother lived nearby, but Lance lives in Boston these days. Anyway, just let my mom know what dates your mom has off from work, and she'll arrange for the flights and everything. I want her to feel like she's part of our family while she's here."

AT EVERY SEPTEMBER KNIGHTS GAME, the cameras show a shot of me watching the game next to Helen and Dan. Jen extends an invitation for me to join her in Arthur's suite for home games, but Sasha thinks the metrics are better if I'm sitting in my "boyfriend's" suite with his parents. It gives the impression that it must be serious since I'm friendly with his friends and family.

Helen and Sasha are both excited to have my mom in

town for a Knights home game. Sasha is already planning the social media posts about our parents meeting each other while Helen is planning spa days and mani-pedis at the salon. My goal is to have my work replacement trained enough to use that first week in October as a test run to see how she does on her own. If she passes, I'll pack up my desk decorations and be free from the most normal and draining part of my life.

It's the third week of the season when I notice that Sasha often streams the broadcast of the game on the local channel to hear the commentary of the game and players. Liam is on a trajectory to beat his past September records for yards. It bodes well for the contract extension conversation that'll happen with the front office when the season ends. He's playing too well with Arthur for the team to even think the words "free agency." If they don't extend his current contract, they'll be clamoring for him to sign a new one that would last until his retirement. First, we need to make it through this season.

"All the people who want to believe in true love think you're the reason Liam is somehow playing better than he ever has," Natalie tells me when we meet for the game a few days before my mom's arrival. "Mostly the wives and girlfriends of the guys who watch football religiously. It's refreshing to see that you have a band of supporters, even if it's somewhat contingent on your husband's football skills."

"Much of my life these days seems to be contingent on my husband's football skills," I say jokingly.

Dan laughs and says, "Don't be silly. He makes more from endorsements and investments than he does from playing for the Knights. He might be one of the highest paid for his position, but he functions as a wide receiver half the time. Wide receivers have been the hot commodity during the last few off-seasons."

I still remember the shock that rippled through the city when the Knights traded away their star wide receiver after narrowly losing the conference championship game in over-time. It was the only time in the last four seasons that the Knights weren't playing in the league championship game. Other teams were signing wide receivers to big contracts while the Knights were negotiating a contract extension with Martin Mound. He wanted more money than the team could offer given the salary cap and other team needs, so they traded him to the team located where Martin spends his off-seasons. Even if the Knights had offered more money, I suspect Martin wanted to leave.

The Knights entered the next season with rookies at the starting positions on both offense and defense, and fans were hopeful and hesitant about the rebuilding. What started as a rebuilding season ended with a championship parade. Those wins made it apparent that Arthur didn't need Martin as much as he needed Liam. Arthur can survive without Liam, but the few times my husband has missed a game, his absence is evident on the offense.

I PACE the terrazzo floors of the new terminal at the Kansas City International Airport, waiting for my mom's plane to land. Helen and I made the trip to pick her up because Liam is at Arthur's house for a team dinner tonight. I'm just relieved that Liam didn't offer to host sixty men on the same night that my mother is flying into town. Imagine introducing them all to my mother, who is still a catch, while stumbling over the first names of the players I haven't memorized yet. The rookies are too young and too new to have been on my watchlist before marrying Liam, and the married players weren't on there at all by default.

The arrivals board updates my mom's flight status to "landed." I had been tracking the flight on my phone, and the plane took off an hour later than scheduled. Commercial flights are unpredictable these days between a shortage of staff and any number of maintenance issues on top of the weather conditions that planes have always battled. There's a constant concern that a flight might be canceled rather than just delayed by those aforementioned hurdles.

Helen had parked the car in the parking garage across the street from the main entrance so that we could wait inside the terminal rather than circling the cell phone lot. She's on her phone taking care of things for Liam while I continue my back and forth across the length of the area. Natalie had a hand in some of the local artwork selections when preparing for this infrastructure upgrade.

I hear the click of her heels before I turn around and see the woman who gave up her dreams to raise me on her own. Despite that she spent hours on a plane, she's flawless from her makeup to her clothes and her hair. The woman looks fit for a different type of runway than the one her plane landed on. As much as I care about my appearance, I draw the line at wearing heels while traveling, but my mother has never let that deter her. It's a wonder she's stayed single all these years given the way men fawn over her.

With her heels on, my mother's height matches mine, and she pulls me into a hug as soon as she's close enough. "Money looks good on you," she whispers in my ear so that Helen can't overhear.

I'm wearing the same clothes I owned before I married Liam, but I don't correct her. Natalie likely bought this shirt for me despite my insistence not to. Apart from bedazzled jerseys, I haven't bought much with the money I married into. It took me weeks just to sort through the clothes I already own. Now that I have a new credit card tied to Liam's account, nothing is stopping me from going on a shopping spree apart from finding the time.

"You must be Helen Cartwright," my mom says as she extends her hand out to shake Helen's. In her typical Helen way, though, she pulls my mom in for a hug instead.

"I am, which makes us family. No need for formalities

with us, Heather," Helen insists, and I can see my mom visibly soften at Helen's warmth. Some people pretend to be nice to hide how mean they are, but Helen is as genuine as they come. My mom is good at a lot of things including keeping people at arm's length and never letting down her walls. If it weren't for the years I spent as Natalie's roommate, I would be as lonely as she is. She hides it well, but I've known her long enough to see beneath the mask.

I roll my mom's suitcase for her as we walk to where Helen's car is parked in the garage. In California, EVs have become a dime a dozen over the last decade. Still, my mom seems impressed by Liam's generosity toward his family. I let my mom have the front passenger seat while I buckle up in the seat behind her. We swing by my and Liam's house first to give her the grand tour.

"I'm surprised Liam still lets you drive that old car of yours," she comments when she sees my Honda Civic parked in one of his garage spots.

"That's on his list of things once the season is over," Helen says as she unlocks the door and deactivates the alarm system. It's news to me. Liam hasn't mentioned my car at all in the weeks we've been together. Usually, we take his car when we go out together, and most of the time, we eat at home because it's easier and healthier. Unless we're already out together for one of his games, it's hard to find the motivation to leave the house after getting home from work. I can't imagine how much harder it is for couples who have kids.

My mom doesn't say much as we show her around the spacious property, but her face expresses more than her words could. If I'd held up a mirror to my face the first time I saw it, she and I would look like twins. After seeing the master suite, my mom slips off her heels, a move that's out of character for her when she's not at home. Helen is better at giving the tour than I am, and I wonder if she missed her calling as a real estate agent. It's a viable option if Liam ever decides he doesn't need her as his assistant anymore.

Though it's dark, we turn on the backyard lights to show my mom the pool and expansive yard. "A guy is coming to winterize the pool tomorrow, so you came at the perfect time to see it," Helen explains to my mom as we walk around the tiled finish. My mother-in-law knows more about what's going on at my house than I do, but that's something I'm hoping to remedy once I'm no longer going to work in an office downtown.

Next to me, my mom yawns from the travel fatigue. California is two hours behind Kansas City, so it's still early for her. Helen notices as well and her eyes meet mine in question. I shrug in response, but my mom is the one to say something first.

"Helen, if you don't mind, I'd like to go to your place to get ready for bed," my mom says. "I wanted to stay and meet Liam tonight, but the airport hassle takes a lot of energy."

In his impeccable timing, Liam walks in from the garage as we head toward Helen's car. Despite his long day, he stands tall and confident when he sees us. He extends his hand to my mom and says, "It's great to finally meet you in person."

"Wow, you're much larger in person than you appear on video calls and television," my mom says as she shakes his hand. Her tone oozes the same flattery she gives to every man we meet who has money. For her, it's so instinctual that she doesn't realize she's doing it now. If Liam notices it, he'll wait until later to point it out to me. Given his profession, he's likely accustomed to the comment when meeting people for the first time. Many don't realize how tall tight ends are until they see one in person.

"I don't want to keep you from the warm bed waiting for you at my mom's house, but I'd love to have lunch with you and Odette while you're here," he says with a smile that would charm any mother. "I want to get to know the woman who raised my incredible wife."

Despite myself, I blush at his compliment. What is this man doing to me?

My mom has an inquisitive expression when she says, "I'd love to hear about your life since you married my daughter. I have to make sure you're as good as you seem to be."

I keep quiet in hopes that this conversation will end swiftly. Helen appears amused at the exchange. My mom yawns again before she hugs me goodnight and leaves with Helen. Once my mother is no longer in view, Liam's exhaustion becomes apparent. Around me, he doesn't hide how tired he is, but he put on a show for my mother.

"I want full honesty from you. On a scale of one to ten, how excited are you that she's here?" He asks me as we walk to our bedroom.

"It's too early to say," I reply before brushing my teeth. I'm not usually this avoidant, but my mother invokes mixed emotions. She's the biggest influence on my perspective of the world, and I'm seeing both the positive and negative aspects of that. Children who grow up with both parents around like Liam did become a balance of both perspectives, but I didn't have a second viewpoint to balance out that of my mother's.

Knowing that I need a minute to process my emotions, Liam waits for me to finish. It's difficult to have a conversation while both of us are brushing our teeth and flossing. I never would have thought that flossing could be attractive, but seeing a man who takes care of his teeth is more appealing than I previously gave it credit for.

"Did you take a shower before you went to the airport to pick up your mom, or do you need to do that now? I showered at the training facility before going to Arthur's," he says before swishing mouthwash.

"Her flight was an hour late, so I had time to shower," I say before retreating to the walk-in closet to change into my pajamas. "I'm happy that she's here, but I'm also nervous of her reaction to the football world. She was part of the basketball world for years and got burned by the worst of it. Part of her might be concerned due to her experience with a professional athlete."

Due to his height and long legs, Liam is behind me in only a few strides. He pulls me close to him and kisses the top of my head to silently reassure me. No matter how strong I am or how thick my walls are, he sees straight to the heart of my insecurities. I know he isn't my father, but it doesn't erase the effects his abandonment has had on me and my mother. Her appearance with me at the game on Sunday might spark questions in the media about my father, and we both need to be prepared for that.

"Is it weird that I think your mom is hot for her age?" Liam says to incite a laugh and break me out of my thought spiral.

I roll my eyes and reply, "You and every other guy who meets her. It's annoying, but it's also nice because I have her genetics. If you play your cards right, you're going to have a hot wife twenty to thirty years from now."

"It's nice to know that I won't have to marry someone that much younger than me to reap that benefit," he teases. "No need to divorce and marry a younger woman if you're married to someone who hardly ages. I know that you insist it doesn't bother you, but I think your dad missed out on the best things he could have had by not being around for you and your mom. No career is worth giving up a family for."

I kiss his cheek and slip out of his arms to finish getting ready for bed. I might not have to work tomorrow, but he has another full day of training and practice. He relents because he knows I'm pulling away for his sake. Without the constraints of time and responsibility, I would let him spend hours making me forget about everything outside of us. Until the bye week, we have to think about games and practices and the team most nights. Liam's body needs rest from the extreme exertion he puts it through six days of the week. Seeing this side of things, it's a wonder how my parents dated with how both their schedules would have demanded this level of physical demand.

●

"I've had my eye on the social media sites for some of the articles about you two," my mom says when Liam joins us for lunch. "It's interesting how invested people are in the lives of professional athletes. I'm glad we didn't have that and smartphones when I was your age and in that world."

"It certainly adds an element to things that didn't exist when the professional sports leagues started decades ago," Liam says as he waves over our waiter. He's already told my mom that he's taking care of her meal, and she claimed she didn't want to take advantage of his generosity. It's her way of seeming like she doesn't expect to be treated even though it's exactly what she expects. My husband is too much of a gentleman to let his mother-in-law pay for lunch.

We each order a special from the lunch menu at Q39 before the waiter leaves us again. Kansas City is world-renowned for its barbecue, but it's up for debate about which local restaurant has the best. My favorites are Q39 and Joe's Kansas City, but some prefer Jack Stack, Gates, Slaps, or one of the others. There are annual barbecue competitions, and now restaurants can compete for a one-year spot in the airport terminal. That and jazz are what Kansas City has been known for over the years. Lately, sports are becoming part of the city's overall appeal to tourists with the rise of the Knights and the women's soccer stadium nearing its opening game.

My mom takes a sip of her martini before she asks Liam, "How many more years do you think you'll play before retirement?" I hold in my groan at her question. Sportscasters have been talking about this since the end of last season.

"That depends on how long I can keep playing well while staying healthy," he says with ease. "It will also depend on how contract negotiations go with the Knights front office in the off-season. They know I don't want to move, and I'm not concerned about the money side of it as much as some think I should be. I'd rather have the wins and the glory over the largest contract. It's about legacy and community for me."

I expect the woman who raised me to comment how the money will matter when he retires, but instead, she says, "It's refreshing to hear someone playing in professional sports who cares more for the team than he does personal gain. Legacy is what will earn the endorsements that bring cash flow when you leave the field. I think you're being smart about it."

"Even if it's not smart, it's where my heart is. I wouldn't be who or where I am if I sold my soul for the bigger contract. It helps that I have my mom around to keep me grounded." Liam Cartwright is a better man than the gossip sites show, and now my mom sees the heart of gold that I married without knowing. My gold-digger tendencies were aiming for the bank account, not the heart. It's disorienting knowing he's as good as he seems.

My mother inspects him and dissects his words. This is the moment she's sure I didn't marry an athlete like my father, and it softens her. "I'm looking forward to seeing you play in person."

◦

I THOUGHT I had seen it all until my mother and Helen showed up in matching Liam Cartwright jerseys. I'm wearing one of my bejeweled versions, the sparkle being the only thing setting me apart from my two mothers. For once, my mother wears sneakers instead of heels.

When she sees me eyeing her footwear, she says, "Helen convinced me to leave the heels at home since there's a chance of rain in the forecast. I don't want to take the chance of getting my red pumps wet."

In Kansas City, the chance of rain on the weather forecast

115

is up for interpretation. While storms can roll in quickly from any direction, the best way to guess is to look at the sky. My weather app might say it's only a 20% chance, but the darkening clouds foretell otherwise. Lightning will delay the game, but rain alone isn't enough to stop the action on the field. Some welcome the opportunity to play in the rain while others wish Camelot Stadium had a canopy or dome. If I weren't too recognizable to sit in the stands, I wouldn't mind experiencing the warm rain. The cold rain is what I avoid.

The Cartwright suite is lively with Dan joining in on the action. Natalie walks in holding a pizza she snagged from the owner's suite. On the green space below, the fans are restless at the prospect of a downpour from the heavens. To add to the drama, this late afternoon game is against a division rival. The skies hold back for the first quarter, but during the second, the rain comes. The natural grass field holds up long enough against the elements to last to halftime without incident. During halftime, lightning puts the game on a longer pause than scheduled.

"They're delaying the game until the lightning subsides," Sasha informs us as she taps furiously at her phone. "Based on the radar, it shouldn't be much longer than another fifteen minutes or so. The storm is passing quickly enough."

Next to me, my mom and Helen scroll through social media on their phones for mentions of my mother's visit. The cameras find me and Helen at some point in every game now. It won't take much for the public to piece together our additional guest's relation to me. When I look over at my mom, her face has gone pale.

"What's wrong?" I ask her quietly. Her phone displays a shot of the three of us in the suite during the second quarter of the game. Whatever is spooking my mother, Sasha has caught onto it and taps my shoulder with a gesture that we should discuss things away from the viewing level. My mother joins us in the back corner.

"Heather, do you want to tell her, or should I?" Sasha asks

my mother. I just want to know what could be going on that's so surprising.

My mom takes a deep breath and says, "Your father commented on the photo of us. He might not have recognized you before, but now that he's seen us together, he knows that you're his daughter. It's nothing revealing or incriminating though."

"It is something that we'll want to monitor," Sasha says carefully. "Due to his own fame and influence in the sports world, it could cause a ripple effect. Odette told me that she had never known or met her father. Heather, have you had any contact with him recently? Anything he could use as blackmail against you or your daughter?"

"He's the one who walked out of our lives," my mother says with less strength than usual. "I told him that the door is always open if he wants to have a relationship with Odette, but he's never made an effort to do so. Do you think that he'll reach out now that he knows her connection to a well-known professional football player?"

Sasha, who multitasks scrolling through social media while having this conversation, takes a moment to respond. "I think that anything is possible. Unlike some athletes, he's done well for himself following retirement. Sometimes, professional athletes find themselves bankrupt after they stop playing and the endorsements dwindle. Your father continues to do well for himself as a commentator."

It's not lost on me that they both know who my father is while I'm the one left in the dark. Sasha must have gotten his name from my mother when I wasn't around for her to know to look out for something like this. Would I even recognize his name if I scrolled through the comments of me and my mother? I've never followed basketball to the same degree as football, baseball, and soccer since Kansas City doesn't currently have a professional basketball team; however, sports are an easy icebreaker to spark a conversation with men. I decide that it's time to stop avoiding that part of who I am.

"What's his name?" I ask both of them but mostly my mother.

She gives me a wry smile and says, "Percy Donovan."

I hardly remember the remainder of Liam's game as my mind mulls over the man responsible for half my genetic makeup and much of how my mother raised me after his exit from our lives.

RULE #8

First class or bust (unless it's a private plane)

SAYING goodbye to the full-time job I'd had since moving to Kansas City was harder than I anticipated. Jack's niece doesn't need me when I return to the office after my mother's visit, but I continue to oversee her until it's time to leave for Germany. I use the few weeks of transition to ease my way out by going to the office a few days a week while also arriving late and leaving early on those days. Without battling the rush hour traffic, going into the office is less stressful, and Liam notices.

"I'm not used to your being home when I leave for practice," he says as he kisses me goodbye. "It makes it harder to leave you versus the empty house."

"I'm leaving in half an hour," I say while rolling my eyes. "That's hardly enough time for what you have in mind."

He mocks offense as he says, "What if I just want to sit and have a conversation with my wife about her feelings since finding out who her father is? Not everything that goes through my head is about sex."

I raise my eyebrows, refusing to entertain the can of worms we would be unleashing if we were to have that conversation before work. "We can talk about that over dinner tonight," I promise despite myself. He's waited until my mom was back in Los Angeles to bring it up. Today is when he's forcing me to stop avoiding the topic of my birth father.

He kisses me again before he groans and hurries to his car. Once he's in the driveway, I concoct a plan to distract him when he gets home from work.

◉

"I CLEARED it with Coach Wes for you to fly with us for the Germany game," Liam tells me as we eat the steak and roasted potatoes prepared by Jeff. "My mom was watching the prices for a first-class seat as a backup, but it would have sucked to be on different planes for a transatlantic flight both ways."

> Rule #8: First class or bust (unless it's a private plane)

"What does it matter if we're on separate planes if we're likely to be sleeping the whole time? Isn't a sleeping pod the whole point of being in first class for a long flight?" I tease. "You're the one who will be surrounded by all your teammates. I would have to convince Natalie to take time off to fly to Germany with me so that I'm not stuck next to a stranger for the whole flight."

He chews on his steak and mulls over his response. "You would have had a layover somewhere on the East Coast as well while the team's chartered plane is a direct flight. That adds at least three additional hours to your travel time one way. The Kansas City Airport doesn't have any direct flights to Europe yet."

"Don't remind me," I say as I cut the remainder of my steak into bite-sized cubes. I'm careful not to get any food on the fluffy robe I put on over my outfit underneath. I'm prepared to utilize my secret weapon if he tries to talk about my father tonight. So far, we've steered clear of the need.

"The moment they start direct flights to Europe again, I'm taking you on one," he says. "As long as it's not during training camp or football season, that is."

Willing to keep him talking about traveling, I quip, "At the rate the league is scheduling games in Europe, it may not matter if it's during the season or not. Didn't the team in Jacksonville just play in London multiple weeks in a row?"

"I do not envy them, although getting time to explore the city on my day off would be a nice perk," he confesses. "It's been a few years since the last time the Knights played in London, but I've heard the fans there lately are as energetic as the fans in Kansas City. Makes sense when you see how crazy the soccer fans are over there."

"Have you seen how crazy the soccer fans are here? Natalie and I went to one of the watch parties during the women's international soccer tournament. That experience supports why Kansas City is trying to claim the title of the Soccer Capital of America."

Liam typically eats slower than me, but tonight he's cleared off his plate faster than I can. "I know you're only bringing up soccer to avoid talking about your dad. You can't fool me, Odette."

"But I can entice you," I say as I untie my robe to reveal his large jersey that's long enough to pass as a short dress.

He takes a sharp breath and closes his eyes. "If you're not wearing anything under that, you win this time."

"Do I come across as an amateur when it comes to distracting you?" I ask in a challenge. In a few swift movements, he sweeps me up in his arms to carry me to our bedroom. My plot to distract him proves to be a success for today, but tomorrow I'll have to let Liam into my thoughts and feelings about my father.

"Let me into your head," he says in request as we chop vegetables together the next night. "I want to know the good and the bad. I'm not going to judge you or hold anything you say against you."

So, I open the floodgates. "It's frustrating that he's had decades to reach out to me or my mom, but he waits until we're trending on social media to leave a comment on a photo. It's as if he forgot we existed until he saw a photo of us together and learned that his only daughter is married to one of football's best tight ends. I understand that he was young and didn't know how to balance the demands of being a star athlete while having a family. He could have reached out when he retired from playing. The only upside is that he doesn't have a wife and family that he replaced us with." Once the words are out, I feel the weight of them lift from my chest.

"I don't know Percy, so I can't speak for him," Liam begins, "but sometimes men tend to avoid situations that make them feel like they failed. The reason he never tried may be that he feels like he failed you and your mom by not being there from the beginning. It's an unhealthy avoidance tactic. No one likes to feel like they're lacking in an area of their lives. He was also young and dumb given that he was under twenty-five. It's scientifically proven that the brain's frontal lobes aren't fully formed until the mid-twenties."

"Where's the 'all your feelings are valid' part of that speech?" I joke to ease the seriousness.

Liam leans over to quickly kiss the top of my head. "I'm always on your side. While he likely has his reasons, you're the one who didn't get a choice in how he treated you by not being there. I respect and admire the life you and your mom built for yourselves despite that. It's not my place to tell you whether you should or shouldn't let him into your life now if he expresses interest. My only suggestion is that either way, don't make the decision based on your hurts or his mistakes. Decide from a place of forgiveness and healing. I had a hard time when my parents separated, but I had to release them both from the expectations I'd held onto. They don't owe me anything after all they've done for me."

"You're right," I relent as I cipher through his words. "My mom hasn't mentioned anything since that initial comment, so it could be a one-time occurrence. Do you think it's strange that neither of my parents got married to other people?"

"Neither of my parents have even dated other people during their separation. Have you ever asked your mom why she hasn't gotten married? I find it hard to believe that she hasn't had men try to win her over."

Though my mom always encouraged me to find someone financially well-off and marry him, she's never tried to do the same for herself. She's had a few boyfriends here and there, but she's never accepted any of their proposals. I only know about them because I would catch her coming home late with one of them while I was home on school break. Before I left for boarding school, she didn't bother dating at all.

"Maybe my mom is secretly a romantic, and I never knew it," I joke as I drizzle olive oil over the vegetables. "Romantics are picky about who they choose to spend the rest of their lives with, for better or for worse."

Liam opens the oven for me as I slide the tray of veggies onto the top rack. "Which part is for better or for worse though, the marriage or being picky? What if I'm one of those picky romantic people?"

"You proposed to me on what doesn't even count as a first date," I remind him. "'Love at first sight' might be romantic, but it doesn't sound picky to me."

"It's about as picky as you can be because it's all up to an illusive sense of knowing someone without really knowing them," he argues. "It's exclusive in that it weeds out the women I merely find attractive and narrows it down to whether or not I can see a future with that woman in just a glimpse of her. It might not be the smartest way to choose a life partner, but it's certainly more adventurous. Besides, over half of people surveyed say they've experienced what they believe to be 'love at first sight.'"

I'm incapable of hiding my shock at that fact. "I knew people in general weren't logical, but over half? I mean, I knew I was attracted to you. That doesn't mean that I've been in love with you from the moment I saw you that night."

"It was my kiss that did it." I lightly punch him, and he gives me a smile that would make any woman fall for him at first sight. There's a difference between an initial strong attraction and being certain of a lifetime commitment. Unless your name is Liam Cartwright.

THE PLAYERS whose wives are staying home with their children say goodbye to us at the airport before we board the chartered plane en route to Frankfurt, Germany. Jen is among those kissing her husband goodbye while corralling the kids to hug their dad before he leaves for a long weekend. It's a quick turnaround with little time to sightsee, but Liam wants me with him for all of it. Of the wives and girlfriends, only six of us join the players for the international game of the Knights season. Upon second look, all of us are wives. Marriage to a player might be a requirement for this particular flight.

"Is Jen going to survive the weekend alone with your two kids?" I ask Arthur as he takes the seat on the other side of Liam. With how large most of the football players are, the team had to charter a plane with a higher ratio of first-class and business-class seats. Only a handful of them could even fit in the economy class seats that keep shrinking. Soon only children will be able to sit in them comfortably.

"My mom is watching the kids for the weekend while Jen has a girls' weekend in New York," Arthur says as he inspects the cleanliness of the sleeping pod. I could smell the cleaning products when we walked onto the airplane, so I'd be surprised to find a spec of dust anywhere. "If I weren't flying back to KC with the team, I would just fly straight to New York from whatever airport in Europe has an open first-class seat. My mom would kill me if I left her by herself to fly with the kids out to the Hamptons to meet us, though."

I try to put together the moving pieces in my mind. "Wait, is Jen staying out there?"

Arthur nods. "It doesn't make sense for her to fly home only to fly back that way the next day. Plus, the kids love spending time with grandma. I'm sure Helen would be willing to do the same for you two when you decide to have kids."

Liam squeezes my knee as if he can't wait to start having kids with me as soon as I'm ready. He doesn't say it, but it's no secret that he wants a family. Meanwhile, my brain finally remembers what I forgot to pack—my birth control pills. I spent days trying to figure out what time I should take them to ensure I could keep it around the same accounting for the time difference in Germany. At least, Liam is good about doubling up on our protection. He has no intentions of knocking me up before I'm ready. What he doesn't know is that I'm not sure I'll ever feel ready to be a mother. I still wrestle with whether I'm sure about a future with him.

Matt, the placekicker, and his wife Melanie sit in the row behind us. I haven't had the chance to talk to either of them much before now.

"Don't let him pressure you into having kids," Melanie says, having overheard the last part of our conversation. "It's not a race. Yes, there's a biological timeline, but you still have a good ten years as long as you're not planning on giving birth to a whole football team. None of us need to feel pressure to keep up with Arthur and Jen. Being a football wife is enough to get used to during the first season or two without adding a baby to the mix."

"I agree with everything my wife just said," Matt adds succinctly. "Plus, I don't envy the days that Arthur shows up to practice sleep-deprived because one of the kids kept him up. The fans wouldn't take too kindly to my missing field goals because I'm exhausted."

Arthur defends himself with, "Practices and games are only a fraction of how we spend our lives. What's the point of having that if you don't have a wife and kids to share it with? My favorite part about being a football league champion is getting to share the victory with my kids, even if they don't yet fully understand the grit and hard work it took to get there."

Melanie chimes in, "I'm trying to convince Matt that we can try to time it so that I give birth during the early part of the off-season. That way, he doesn't have the worry or tiredness of being a new father on his mind while making those field goals."

While Arthur shares the story of his second child being born during the season, Liam and I tune out of the conversation to have a private one of our own using our phones connected to the plane's Wi-Fi.

> Remember how I said I thought I forgot something? My birth control pills are in the vanity drawer at home

LIAM

> We'll be fine for a few days. I didn't forget anything, and it's only a few days. Besides, it's not the end of the world if you get pregnant. We're already married, even if the media doesn't know that yet.

> You seem to be forgetting that we haven't even known each other for more than a few months. Better safe than sorry. Unlike you, I have self-control

> Fine, fine. You're right. No need to rush things. I promise to be good.

"Are you two texting while sitting beside each other?"

Arthur asks, leaning over to spy on Liam's phone. "On second thought, I don't want to see what you two probably send each other that you don't want us to hear. I'm just glad I won't have to share a room with Liam this time. We would always get grouped on games that Jen can't go to."

"Who is your roommate this time?" Liam asks as he locks his phone screen. It's his way of signaling our return to the group conversation.

Arthur practically beams, "Since there's an odd number of us, I get a room to myself."

"Oooo, I'll trade you if you really want to share with Liam for old time's sake," I jokingly offer, and Liam mocks offense. "Actually, scratch that. I like a warm bed, and Liam's a human space heater."

"You heard it here first," Liam says as if he's telling a breaking story. "Odette Cartwright married the talented and handsome tight end Liam Cartwright for his body heat, not his good looks or his money."

I add to the act. "Babe, we both know that I married you for your tight end."

"That's about the only football position that can be used as an innuendo," Melanie says thoughtfully, and the men proceed to go through each one, debating on whether Long Snapper would fit the bill.

Eventually, we eat dinner before we take advantage of our sleeping pods to rest up for the bustling city that awaits.

RÖMERBERG, the historical market square, is the type of architecture I expected to see in the German city. What I didn't anticipate are the skyscrapers that are also part of Frankfurt's makeup. It's a jarring combination that somehow blends in a way that a modernized European city would have to in this era. If a growing city isn't expanding out, it has to build up. American cities these days are doing both at differing rates, Kansas City included.

Though the game is a few days away, the fans' excitement is tangible. Our entourage checks into our hotel for the duration of our stay to rest up for a few hours before a press conference scheduled for later in the afternoon. Sunday's opponent, the Seagulls, arrived yesterday and are staying at a hotel nearby. While the Knights are settling in for their four-night stay, the Seagulls are touring Deutsche Bank Park in preparation for Sunday's showdown. Tomorrow will be the Knights' turn to view the field and facilities. Due to its main function for football (not the American version), the field is natural grass, to the relief of the Knights players.

Simmering beneath the surface of the usual league drama are rumors that the players' association may require all stadiums to switch to natural grass. With many of the stadiums selected to host games for the 2026 international soccer tournament, some that currently use turf have plans to make the transition. Ahead of the curve, Camelot Stadium switched from turf to grass in the 90s. Like the Knights, the Seagulls are accustomed to playing on real grass.

"I have a strange question," I preface to Liam as he unpacks his suitcase. Assuming he's listening, I continue. "Does your training team look at the schedule and make changes to your regimen or recovery based on which games are on turf versus natural grass?"

He pauses what he's doing to turn and look at me. "How much do you know about the whole turf and grass debate?"

"I know that two quarterbacks this season have torn their Achilles tendon while playing on artificial turf," I state, impressing my husband with my knowledge. "I also know that you tend to play with your injuries as much as you can because you take your recovery as seriously as you take the games."

"I have more inflammation after playing on turf, so it does add another layer to the recovery," he admits as he returns his attention to his suitcase. "As minor as it is in the grand scheme of my career, playing home games on a natural grass field is one of the pros to spending my whole career with the Knights. Free agency comes with the risk of ending up on a team that plays on turf. While games on turf are currently unavoidable, it's less than half because Camelot Stadium accounts for half of them, sometimes more when we're the top seed for the playoffs."

Avoiding turf is a drop in the bucket compared to playing with one of the best quarterbacks and top coaches in the league. Not everyone is best friends with his quarterback. The team culture is a bigger risk than the makeup of the field, but he doesn't need to tell me that. When it comes to his loyalty to Kansas City and the Knights, Liam is an open book.

For us, the rest period consists of showering and room service for lunch. As much as we want to nap, we know the guidelines for jet lag. The game on Sunday is in the early evening in this time zone and the morning back in the States. About an hour before the team needs to leave the hotel for the press conference, Helen calls Liam via video call.

"You look like you should have slept a little more on the plane," she says as she inspects her son through the screen. I nudge my way into view to join the call. "See, Odette doesn't look nearly as sleep-deprived as you appear."

"I can assure you that he slept better on the plane than I did," I inform her. "Liam could sleep through a hurricane."

Helen chuckles, "I wish he had slept that well as a baby. It took playing a sound machine as loud as a hurricane to get him to sleep through the night. Make sure you stay awake until it's night there to acclimate to the time difference. You'll want to be able to get enough sleep. Sunday is a big game for both your European fans and for bragging rights with Martin Mound and the Seagulls."

"Mom, this isn't my first time playing in Europe, nor is it Odette's first time here. We know how jet lag works. We have a press conference in an hour and dinner tonight, so there won't be a chance for us to fall asleep earlier than we should. Coach has us covered."

Helen gives us a tired smile. I wonder how much sleep she got knowing we were on a plane over the Atlantic. "I'm making two pans of lasagna, but I'll put them both in the freezer since you'll be in the Hamptons next week. Any other food requests while I'm taking over your kitchen?"

"Nana's apple pie," Liam says without hesitation. "I don't think I can wait for Thanksgiving."

Helen and I both roll our eyes at his request. "I'll make her apple pie if you win on Sunday," Helen strikes a deal with her son. "In fact, I'll make enough pies for the whole team to have a slice if you win." Helen knows how to bribe these men.

Half an hour later, Liam tells his teammates about his nana's apple pie that awaits as a prize of victory. Beating their former teammate Martin Mound and winning in Germany were already perks, but these men love their apple pie. When the restaurant presents the best food Germany has to offer, I question whether the kitchen will have enough food to keep up with these football players' appetites. I don't doubt that the league or the team is more than compensating them for the extravagant feast. By the time we return to the hotel for the night, Liam and I hardly have the energy to brush our teeth and change before crashing.

ON SUNDAY EVENING, the retractable roof stadium usually filled with football fans is taken over by American football as a sea of red dotted with jerseys of various other colors. On the schedule, this game is designated a home game for the Knights. Given their licensing rights, the Knights have a fan base in Germany that the Seagulls haven't been able to capitalize on yet. If I weren't feeling the lingering jet lag, the atmosphere would fool me into thinking we were at Camelot

Stadium rather than on the other side of the Atlantic. I sit with the other players' wives in a section of Knights season ticket holders who made the trek across the ocean for this game. The majority of the seats are filled with Germans and those from other European countries.

Traditions from both versions of football are incorporated into the experience. If we were staying longer than a few days, I would talk Liam into going to a game for the local club here to see the other side of it. For the first half of the game, the Knights dominate on both offense and defense, giving them a 17-point lead going into halftime.

During the third quarter, the Seagulls adjust and manage to chip away at the lead until they're only down by one touchdown. When it looks like the Seagulls might tie the game to extend it into overtime, the Knights' defense holds them and forces a fourth-down play with less than a minute remaining on the game clock. In the last play, the Seagulls fumble the snap and sabotage themselves. Two hours after the game ends, Helen sends me a photo of all the baking supplies she bought to make pies.

THE LARGE VACATION house we share with the Welch family is beyond anything I stayed in with Natalie. The two of us would never need this much space, but it's ideal for six of us. A house like this is in high demand during peak summer months, but one should never underestimate the beauty of the Hamptons in the fall. Besides, the outdoor temperatures have no bearing on the heated indoor pool in this vacation house.

On the first day, we sleep until noon. Arthur and Jen don't have the same luxury because they have two energetic children who love to swim.

"It's a useful skill, and it burns a lot of their energy," Jen says as I eye both kids wading through the pool with Arthur and Liam by their sides. "Letting them do this for a few hours guarantees that they'll nap and sleep through most of the night. I'm thankful Arthur talked me into having an indoor pool at our house."

"I'm surprised they're not tired of swimming," Arthur says from the water. "Maybe they'll both choose a water sport rather than one on the grass."

I look at their daughter and joke, "That one is destined to be a water polo star. Forget soccer trophies and football championship rings, she's going to have gold medals. Time to invest in more water polo clubs in the Kansas City area."

"Odette, are you going to join us, or are you going to sit there and tempt me with your bikini?" Liam asks when both the kids have their heads under the water.

"I'm observing how you are with children," I say truthfully. Watching him does make the prospect more appealing than it ever has even if it's still a decision for the distant future.

Next to me, Jen is scrolling through social media on her phone. "When did you two have time in Germany to stage a proposal?" She holds up her phone to show the photo of Liam down on one knee and holding a black velvet box in the Palm Gardens.

"Man, your photographer did such a good job," Arthur teases, talking about himself in the third person. "Tell Sasha she owes me one for that."

"We had two hours after their practice and tour of the stadium and before our dinner reservation," I answer Jen's question. "We wore disguises when leaving the hotel to ensure fans didn't recognize us. It's the closest thing to being a celebrity that we're likely to experience."

Ready to join her family in the water, Jen locks her phone and stands. "I'm glad you opted for a destination wedding. Venice in early spring before the flock of tourists takes over. If I didn't love Hawaii so much, I would have gotten married in Italy instead." Jen walks to the deep end of the pool and performs a perfect dive into the saltwater. Compared to them, I'm going to look like an idiot. I know how to swim, but I'm out of practice. Liam and I married too late into the summer for me to get much use of his outdoor pool.

Rather than insisting that I join the rest of them, Liam lifts himself out of the water at the side of the pool and claims the chair Jen wasn't using. Although her mom is in the water, Jen's baby daughter cries in Liam's absence. He knows how to charm all the ladies, even those still in diapers. Arthur pulls his daughter into his arms to calm her while their son wrestles himself onto Jen's back.

"I'm thinking twelve kids is a good number," Liam jokes as he reclines the chair. "A dozen is enough for a whole offense with one substitute."

"What do you think the chances are that all twelve would be boys?" I ask to play along.

"There's no rule against females playing in the league," Arthur yells from the pool, reminding me that our conversation isn't private with these acoustics reverberating every word. "Liam would spoil any daughter of his more than he realizes. I didn't know how bad it was until I had one."

Arthur's words trigger an emotion I've spent decades avoiding. A father is supposed to want to protect and spoil his little girl, not pretend and live his life as if she doesn't exist. Liam senses the shift in my mood.

"Let's go find somewhere to eat lunch," he suggests as he stands and holds his hand out for me, giving me the out I desperately need at this moment.

RULE #9

Don't let emotional attachments make decisions for you

COMING HOME to the drop in temperatures that accompany late fall in Kansas City is like being dunked in cold water. Literally. The highs were still warm during the day when we left, but now it's cold and rainy. It's barely warm enough to keep the precipitation from becoming snow instead. Looking through the window at the pool in the backyard makes me miss summer days in the heat and sunshine. Given his profession, Liam thrives when the weather and the leaves turn. In America, autumn means football season and baseball's championship series. Liam and Arthur return to the training facility while I'm finally sitting still long enough to be confronted by my recent decision to stop working at an office.

I split my time between helping Helen and shadowing Jen. Time with Helen is a long to-do list involving behind-the-scenes aspects of Liam's career. What many don't know or see are the hours he spends with the kids that are helped by his charity. He's as hands-on as his time allows. During the season, it's not as much time as he would like, but Helen steps in when he can't. The kids are just as excited to see her as I imagine they would be if Liam were here himself.

Jen's typical day is different from that of my mother-in-law. Her pace of life has slowed down some since having kids, but she keeps a routine similar to what she had before giving birth to her firstborn. I work out with Jen in her home gym as the kids play in the corner, sometimes with their kid versions of workout equipment. The sports world is going to be watching those two closely since they have two athletes as parents.

Kansas City is home to a professional women's soccer team that's gained a lot of attention lately since Arthur and Jen became part of the ownership group. Spending the day with Jen, I see how she's actively involved in her role in the sport even though she no longer plays professionally. She's paving the way for future generations of women athletes while raising her kids and supporting her husband's career.

Dan flies into town for the Monday night game with plans to stay through the week for Thanksgiving on Thursday. He'll stay for the game the following Sunday before flying home. Liam's brother couldn't take off work for both Monday and Tuesday, but he arrives on Wednesday and is staying through the weekend to attend next weekend's game. It works out that the schedule has home games for the Knights on the weekends before and after the holiday.

This particular game is hyped up more than the typical prime-time showdown because it's a rematch with the team the Knights beat in the league championship game nine months ago. Realistically, it's not a true rematch since some players have been traded or weren't re-signed during free agency, but the sentiment is there. The coaches are the same and the quarterbacks are the same, giving it the feeling of a rematch with lower stakes. If the Knights lose this game, the sting will be less than the sting of losing the championship game would have been.

The private suite is warm and dry while the fans and players are subject to the weather in the open air. Tonight is cold with a relentless drizzle that makes the field just wet enough to keep things interesting. Whoever takes care of the grass on the field deserves a raise, though, because it holds up well when compared to the grass in some of the other football fields. A slight breeze accompanies the rain, but it's not enough to hinder the offense's passing game.

Arthur looks as if he's had extra rest as he effortlessly throws the ball down the field, spreading it out among his various wide receivers and tight ends. It keeps the defense on their toes because he'll throw it to anyone open. Liam has a knack for being the guy who gets open. Each time he makes the catch, the defense is quick to tackle him before he can gain more yardage.

I've seen Liam get tackled countless times while playing the sport he loves, but my breath stops when I witness this hit. Helen and Dan are both silent as we wait. I swear time stops as we watch for the moment that Liam will get up and shake it off. Since the hit involved his head, he'll likely have to come off the field to be checked out by the unaffiliated neurotrauma consultant before they let him back on, but he'll push through it like he always does. Except, he's not getting up. From here, I can't even see if he's moving, and the panic sets in. The training staff and coaches rush onto the field to surround him as the players and thousands of fans pray. I'm as frozen as he is as I wait for them to make a decision or for him to move. Why won't he move and why can't I move? I'm praying under my breath to a God that I hope exists and can hear us in this moment.

"Let's go down to the tunnel," Helen says, and I'm too shocked to wonder how she can be so calm when her son is on the grass not moving. Tall, strong, energetic Liam is still and helpless. On the screens throughout, I watch them carefully lift him onto a stretcher to be wheeled to the waiting ambulance.

"They're going to take him to the sports medicine clinic down the street to do a thorough exam," Dan says to reassure me, but it's anything but reassuring. It's serious enough that they're taking him out of the stadium rather than examining him here. He could have a spinal injury causing permanent paralysis for all we know. As they cart him off, he gives a thumbs up, and my anxiety level drops slightly while applause echoes through the stadium. I'm numb as his parents lead me to their car. Dan drives us to the clinic where they're taking Liam.

How are they functioning as if everything isn't falling apart right now? He's their firstborn son in an ambulance on the way to the emergency room. "Just breathe, in and out," Helen says to me from the front passenger seat. "Worrying about the worst-case scenario only makes it harder. Right now, the only thing we can do is meet him at the clinic and pray on the way there. We can't control the outcome."

I've never been a fan of hospital emergency rooms, not that people enjoy coming here. I push back the barrage of memories from when my grandfather had a heart attack—the heart attack he never recovered from. As if I'm nine again, I hear the echo of my mom's sobs when the doctors deliver the heartbreaking news. My grandfather was the one man who never abandoned us when we needed him. I force myself back to the present, back to the life that still feels new and precarious.

"We're here to see Liam Cartwright," Helen tells the front desk. I wonder if she's experienced this before with her sons. Both boys played multiple sports, and I'd be surprised if neither of them had broken any bones from the years of football.

Another nurse asks, "Are you family?"

"Mom, Dad, and his wife," Helen says in her no-nonsense manner. "If there's a limit on how many guests he can have, his wife Odette should be the one to be with him."

"They're still running tests, but we'll let you know as soon as he's in his room," the nurse says without confirming whether or not all three of us would be allowed to visit him at the same time. At least I can be thankful for the absence of media. Occasionally when a player is transported to the hospital via ambulance, news reporters try to sneak their way in to be the first to get the story.

My phone vibrates with a text notification from Natalie.

Next to me, Helen streams the game from her phone. "He'll want to hear the highlights of the game when he sees us," she says to me as her phone screen shows Arthur throwing a touchdown pass to one of the running backs. The Knights are up by fourteen points now, giving them breathing room and a needed advantage. A few feet away, Dan is on the phone with Lance who is watching the game. From what I can overhear, they're discussing whether Lance should fly into town a day earlier than planned. Is this bad enough to be considered a family emergency?

During the fourth quarter of the game, a nurse calls us back to Liam's room. "The good news is that we've determined it's just a concussion. We'll need to keep him overnight, and he'll need to take it easy for a few days," she explains to us as she leads us through the maze of both tragedy and triumph. In the same hospital building, some are rushed to the operating room while others are wheeled to the delivery room. In a single day, lives begin and end only floors away from one another. In this building though, the focus is specifically on sports injuries to ensure he gets the best care.

If my emotions hadn't gone through the wringer during the last two hours, I would have found it comical to see his tall, muscular body in a hospital gown. Instead, all I feel is relief when his blue eyes find mine. His gaze is as clear as a summer day, and I know that he would run to me to scoop me into his arms if he could. He's hooked up to an IV drip and a heart monitor. When I take a deep breath, it's as if I have been holding mine since watching the defender tackle him on the field. I'm unsettled by the enormity of what I feel as I sit by his side and hold his hand. Seeing that he's okay shouldn't make me feel like I'm finally whole again.

"I might have had my head a little too much into the game today," he tries to joke to break the tension and worry wafting in the air.

"Just because you're wearing a helmet doesn't mean you can't experience short-term or long-term brain injuries," Helen reminds him. This is the reality of dating or marrying a football player that no one likes to talk about. We're aware of the risks of CTE, the advances in technology, and the evolution of the rules and regulations that have been implemented to reduce or prevent it, but it's still a brutal game.

Liam's smile is tired as he tries to reassure us. "It's not as bad as it looked. How are the guys holding up without me?"

Dan checks the live stream on his phone. "You know how those guys are. They've rallied just to show their support. I've already updated your trainers on the diagnosis. By now, it's likely been shared with the reporters and commentators at the game. You're going to be in concussion protocol for at least the next few days."

"Sounds like I chose the perfect week for limited activity," Liam replies with a stronger smile than he wore before. "I didn't want to train during the week of Thanksgiving, anyway. Maybe I can sit and watch a Knights game with my brother for the first time since my rookie year. Imagine actually getting to enjoy my friends and family suite."

"Oh, please, you'll be sitting on the bench with your teammates coaching and cheering them on," Helen points out. If he weren't recovering from an injury, she would have lightly slapped him for his outrageous suggestion. "You won't be able to help yourself if you try to watch from the stands or the suites. By the second quarter, you'll want a headset to point out the weak spots in the opposing team's defense. There's too much of a leader and coach in you to be a spectator when your team is out there."

Though the volume is low, we hear the final whistle that ends the game. The Knights have another win on their record as they steadily march toward the playoffs once again. Before Arthur, the Knights were good enough to earn a berth, but they stalled out in the wildcard games. With Arthur as the quarterback, they kicked off the postseason as the top seed with home-field advantage. Since he's led the offense, they have yet to play a postseason game that isn't the league championship game on any field but their own. In this era, any team in their conference who wants to play in the league championship game has to beat the Knights at Camelot Stadium.

"What does the playoff picture look like now?" Liam asks because football encompasses his life for a good half of the year.

"Knights are still on target to be the top seed," Dan replies, answering what Liam wants to know. "It's going to be tight when looking at the other division leaders, but the Knights have the easiest remaining schedule. If Arthur plays like he did tonight, they don't need you to be 100% until the playoffs."

I know that Dan is hinting to his son not to rush his recovery. Clearing concussion protocol doesn't mean he should be out there getting tackled again right away. It's a father's request to his son to make his health and recovery a priority. If I have to take sides, I'm with Dan Cartwright on this one.

"Coach Anderson, Arthur, and some of the guys are coming by once the post-game conference is over," Helen says as she reads a text from her phone. "Some of the training staff will be over sooner than that. Odette, do you want to stay? I can bring you some food and a change of clothes if you don't want to leave."

"If Liam is here overnight, I should be here with him," I say before the warning bells in my mind can convince me otherwise. It's a decision made from the heart and not the head. Logic tells me to go home, eat, and take a shower because Liam is getting the best care he can whether I'm here or not, but the thought of leaving him causes an ache I have no experience with. All I know is that Liam wants me to stay even though he hasn't asked me to. It's one of the expectations that comes with the ring on my left hand.

Sasha is the first non-family member to find us by Liam's side. Her job requires her to keep her emotions at bay in situations like this. I envy how calm and put together she is despite the day's events. As she approaches, she pauses to take a photo of us with Liam smiling directly at the camera. I don't have it in me to care about how I must look in the picture.

"As much as we hate the head trauma part of the sport, Americans are going to be glad that it's not something more serious," she says as she puts her phone in her pocket to give us her undivided attention. "I've already scheduled some posts about your favorite Thanksgiving meals and traditions, so don't worry about any of your social media stuff. That goes for all of you. Take the time to rest. After I post an update letting people know you're recovering, I'm done until next Sunday."

"I couldn't care less what anyone on the internet is saying right now, anyway," Liam says truthfully. "The only times I've cared lately are when they leave negative comments about the woman they think I'm engaged to."

Sasha brightens at the mention of the engagement post. "Most people have been very receptive to that announcement. A few new endorsements have reached out about possible partnerships with both of you, but those can all wait until the season is over. They were understanding when I told them that with Thanksgiving, Christmas, and playoffs so close together, we'll have to schedule meetings a few months out. Not to mention a destination wedding in the same month as the league championship game."

At the mention of the crazy schedule ahead, Helen says, "Sasha, that's great news, but let's just take this one day at a time right now. Liam's brain is more scrambled than usual at the moment. We can talk about endorsements and social media trends after your week off. If they're seriously interested, they'll wait." Sasha quickly posts the photo she took of us before she makes her exit.

Helen and Dan stay until the athletic trainers arrive. One of them reminds Helen of the steps for concussion protocol. Though Liam is rarely in this position, she knows the process like the back of her hand. I'm the one who doesn't know the ins and outs, but my mind is still recovering from the shock earlier. Dan, the other expert, is staying with us this week for the holiday. Chances are, Liam and I will hardly be alone until the holiday weekend is over. The trainers give me the same spiel they regurgitate to Helen about protocol and player safety. As I watch the large man in the hospital clinic bed, I can't imagine a scenario where I would ever leave his side. That's what scares me. Terrifyingly vulnerable and not at all what I thought I was signing up for when I agreed to marry him. I was agreeing to comfort and financial stability, not to feel like my heart went through the wringer as he was strapped to a stretcher.

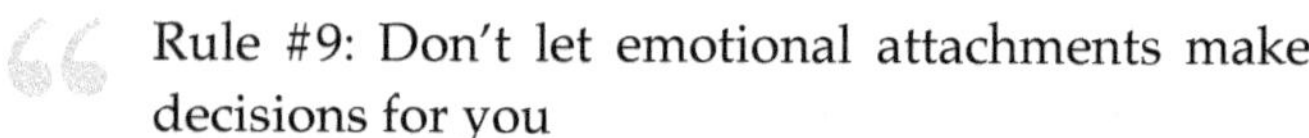

Rule #9: Don't let emotional attachments make decisions for you

When Arthur walks into the room, I excuse myself to take a walk and get some air. Knowing those two need alone time is the perfect escape. The wedding planning is still early enough to cancel and get refunds for ninety percent of what he's spent. Although I technically have a replacement at the office, it'll be busy enough after the first of the year that I could ask for my job back without taking work away from Jack's niece. My room in Natalie's apartment is likely still vacant with how picky she is about roommates. I can walk out of this clinic and call an Uber right now. I can go home and pack up my things and be out of Liam's house and

Liam's life and Liam's family. I can cut the ties now before we become more entangled in the mess we created by getting married on the same night we met. My heart will hurt being away from him, but I can learn to live with the separation.

Instead, I round the corner and walk back to the room where my husband is recovering from a concussion because I can't leave him while he's in that state. I'm not cruel enough to abandon him while he's taking a temporary—albeit mandatory—break from the career that he loves. I'm not cruel enough to cause a potential rift in his family only days before an American holiday centered around family and friends. I don't even know if it's too cruel to leave in the middle of the best season of his career when his future contract hinges on his performance.

By the time I'm in the hallway outside his room, half the Knights football team is waiting for a turn to see and encourage one of their offensive leaders. Coach Anderson is among them, giving Liam a similar speech to the one Dan gave about prioritizing his health over a quick return. While being a professional athlete can be competitive when it comes to contracts and roster spots, when push comes to shove, they support and respect each other. These men win together and lose together, and Liam celebrates today's win with them even though he couldn't play through to the end.

I stand in the hallway and observe as various teammates show him replays from the parts of the game that he missed. Arthur's eyes meet mine, and he slips out of the room to come talk to me.

"This isn't the norm," he attempts to reassure me. I should probably peek at my reflection to see if I look as drained from this as I feel. "Ideally, a player should never have to be in this position at all. After all the controversy surrounding the Seagulls player last season, the league and players' association have been more strict about checking players following tackles and hits involving the head."

"It's just part of the game, right?" I say hoarsely, my voice tired from being on the brink of an emotional breakdown for hours.

Arthur looks at me thoughtfully. "You know, I wasn't sure about you two. You undoubtedly make him happy and all that, but I wasn't sure whether you feel as strongly for him as he feels for you. I see it now, though. You love him, and you care about his wellbeing. That's why you're struggling to reconcile the worst parts of this sport with the best parts that help him feel like he has a purpose. Just remember, he won't always be in this world at this level. There will be a season that's his last before he moves on to the next passion or the next mountain to conquer. He'll recover faster than you realize, and he'll be on the field again but with more caution. Now that he has you, he has a reason outside himself to recover and take care of himself for the life he'll have after football."

Love. Is this what love feels like? It's not the butterflies of infatuation or the electric desire to be alone with him at night. I'm emotionally drained from the terror and anxiety of imagining the worst-case scenarios of paralysis and Liam never getting to do the things he's the most passionate about. I feel as if I slayed the dragon of worry that my husband's dream could die in that instant, and it's left me raw. It could have been worse. There was a player last season whose heart stopped beating on the field, and they had to perform CPR on the field to revive him. In the face of death, I love that man enough to fight it with him. That is my problem. When he asks one of the running backs to find me, I return to his side with Arthur next to me.

HELEN AND DAN take care of everything from picking up Liam's car and belongings from the stadium to driving us home when the clinic discharges him after observing him overnight. They drop us off at the house before venturing to the grocery store to stock up for Thanksgiving dinner and pick up my mom from the airport. Our full-size freezer is packed with apple pies and two pans of lasagna courtesy of my mother-in-law. Though I'm desperate to shower and change, I let Liam claim the bathroom first since he went from being covered in a layer of sweat to lying in a hospital gown. I preheat the oven for the lasagna and sit in the living room with a cappuccino warming my hands.

Liam emerges from our master suite as the oven reaches the temperature on Helen's instructions. I rush to the kitchen to stop him from trying to put it in the oven himself. "I have strict orders from your mother not to let you do anything for yourself today," I say as I gently shove him out of the way to grab the pan. I slide it onto the top rack and turn around to face him with my arms crossed.

"You confiscated my phone and my tablet," he complains. "What am I supposed to do to keep myself from going stir-crazy? Concussions are the worst."

"I'm just following the guidelines from your doctors and trainers. This is the fastest way to reach full recovery. The less cognitive energy you exert, the more energy you'll have later when our parents are here." The less energy I exert trying to convince him to take it easy, the more patience I'll have later when my mother and mother-in-law delve into wedding planning. It's easy when the decision is mine, but they've been waiting to go over the guest list in person rather than sporadic texts when my mom has downtime on set.

Liam sulks to the couch in the living room where I've drawn the curtains to reduce the natural light. The cloud coverage assists in my efforts to aid in his recovery. "I wanted to invite all the guys over for apple pie today, but having that many football players in one house is the type of loud noise and over-stimulation I'm supposed to avoid."

I sit next to him and hold his hand, letting him lean on me. This is the opposite of disentangling myself from his life. This is attachment and devotion. I push down the fear that tempts me to run and dig in my heels. When things are better, I can think about leaving.

◍

FORTUNATELY, Thanksgiving is one of Liam's better days. Due to his desk job, Lance doesn't have the same muscle bulk as Liam, but the two are the same height with the same blue eyes as Dan. He keeps his questions to himself as he looks between Liam and me. If Liam hadn't been in concussion recovery, the conversation would have been interesting. Liam has been tight-lipped about how much his brother knows of our relationship. The four Cartwrights are typically loud and boisterous when together, but this year is subdued due to the two new family members at the table.

"I thought my hours at the office were bad, but I've never considered how long filming days can be," Lance says after hearing about the movie my mom recently worked on. "It's a wonder how actors find time to memorize their lines let alone sleep."

"I might be out of a job if some of them got enough sleep," my mom jokes. "Hollywood is not for the faint of heart. I've considered switching to theater makeup and moving to New York, but I hate winter enough to keep me in Southern California. Where is it that you live, Lance?"

Lance takes a sip of water before answering. "I've been living in Boston for the last two years. I like it there, but I don't know if it's where I want to stay long-term. I prefer the colder months and snow to the scorching heat of the desert. If I decide to move, I'll probably try Minneapolis next. They get a fair amount of snow in winter, and it's closer to Kansas City."

"Only a six-hour drive," Helen says as if she's the one who's been planting the idea in her son's head. She has a subtle way of hinting her desires to the men around her.

"The real estate market is likely more affordable in the

146

Twin Cities when compared to Boston," Dan adds his own opinion into the mix.

I wonder whether Lance's nomadic habit of moving cities every few years is his way of being different from his football star brother or if he hasn't found a place that makes him want to grow roots and stay. With how connected the world is now, it's a wonder he hasn't tried living in Europe or New Zealand. I can picture Lance in both a coffee shop in Italy and on a safari in the African savanna. Then again, I can envision Liam in those scenarios as well. If Lance weren't leaving on Monday morning, I would try to set him up with Natalie just to see if they would hit it off. Then, I think better of it because if Lance and Natalie started dating, it would make it nearly impossible to let go of Liam when the time comes. If I can figure out how.

If Camelot Stadium didn't have the reputation for being the loudest outdoor stadium, Liam would have joined his team on the sidelines without his jersey, pads, and helmet. Though he's improved some over the last few days, he decides not to risk the loud volume and opts to watch the game from the suite with us. His left knee bobs as he watches his teammates struggle against their opponent.

Under his breath, I hear Liam say, "Calm down, Arthur. You need to slow down and play smart instead of fast."

"I was hoping to get to see you play while I'm here, but getting to watch with you is a fair trade-off," Lance says when the Knights punt the ball on the fourth down. He knows Liam well enough not to talk during the third-down play.

"I wouldn't say getting concussed is a fair trade-off," Liam jokes, but his frustration simmers underneath the comment. If he had his way, he would be out on the field encouraging and energizing his teammates. Arthur has been struggling to find an open receiver so far in this game. The defense and special teams are what's giving the Knights offense a chance to come alive and maybe win this. Field goals might put points on the board, but they don't make for an interesting game unless it's what can tie or win the game in the final seconds of the fourth quarter.

Natalie joins us after the first quarter, greeting Liam with a high-five. She says, "On the bright side, seeing them struggle without you guarantees you'll be offered either a contract extension or a new contract once this season is over."

"What does it matter if we can't do what it takes to claim our spot in the playoffs?" Liam mumbles quietly enough that only I hear him. Only one team in the conference has a higher winning record than the Knights, but that team is entering their bye week and will be tied with the Knights again assuming we win this game and the next. Two other teams, including the Seagulls, have the same record, but the Knights beat both teams earlier in the season.

When the offense walks onto the field during the second quarter, it's like looking at a completely different team than the one that was out there less than an hour ago. Arthur had started the game rushing to get the ball out of his hands, resulting in either dropped passes or receivers who were tackled at the line of scrimmage or after gaining only a yard or two. The only reason to rush is if a defender is barreling towards him, and there wasn't much of that happening with how well the offensive linemen were keeping him protected. This version of Arthur is calm and patient as if he's remembered that he can trust his teammates to give him enough time to get the plays they need to move down the field. Not only that, but part of what makes it difficult for defenders is Arthur's ability to scramble when he does escape the pocket. He can rush and dodge to get the yards they need.

By the time the game reaches halftime, the Knights have tied the game. Though the scoreboard says it's any team's game, the way the Knights have turned the momentum in the second quarter points to another victory for them in Camelot Stadium. When the players return for the second half, they continue in the current that keeps the Knights as the second seed in the playoff picture. Liam's tense shoulders relax when the game officially ends. It wouldn't have mattered where we watched the game; the stress of that game has likely given him a headache.

"How are you feeling?" I ask him as we make the trek from his suite to the parking lot. Based on how tightly he's holding my hand, I sense that he's in some pain.

"Can we have silence on the drive home?" His voice masks some of his physical discomfort. Some, but not all.

"Absolutely." Just as I had on the way to the stadium, I hop in the driver's seat of his SUV. It was comical how much I had to adjust the seat to drive it here. The default setting is for a nearly six-and-a-half-foot-tall man, but his car is new enough and fancy enough to have options for multiple saved seat settings. I claim the second spot for my configurations since Helen prefers to drive her car. Compared to my sedan, Liam's vehicle is bigger than I'm comfortable with. I would struggle without the safety sensors and cameras to help me guide us home.

At a stoplight, I glance over at Liam, unable to see his eyes through his sunglasses. Seeing how just watching the game triggered his headaches, I'm thankful that he made the wise decision to sit this game out. Even if he had tried, the trainers wouldn't have cleared him. Though I have a million questions about how he's feeling, I honor his request for silence as I navigate us back to his house where Dan and Lance will be staying for one more night before flying out tomorrow.

When I pull the SUV into the garage, Liam says, "The worst part about injuries like this is the inability to control my recovery. When I pull a muscle or sprain an ankle, there are stretches I can do to get back on the field quicker, but this is the opposite in a way. The less I do, the better off I am. It's a struggle because I'm not wired to sit and wait."

I turn off the engine before gently holding Liam's hand between both of mine. "The worst of it is over. I know it's hard for you because you're not back all the way yet, but I can see how much you've progressed over the past week. I'm no expert, but I think you'll be back on the field by next weekend."

"You're right, and I'm making it worse by letting the stress get to my head. It feels like there's so much riding on this season," he admits as he takes off his sunglasses with his free hand. It's those words that confirm what my gut has been dreading—I have to stay until at least the end of the season, whether it's Week 18 or the championship game.

December into early January is when a good team begins to hit their stride that will take them to the playoffs. The Knights are facing the opportunity to be the first back-to-back league champions in twenty years. Though Liam doesn't listen to the commentary, the team is aware of the whispers questioning whether or not the Knights are on the brink of dynasty status. Being who he is, my husband is more concerned about the team than he is about his contract negotiations.

When we walk inside the house, Dan and Lance already have leftovers heated up and waiting for us to join them. Liam's mood lifts at the sight of his support system for the last week. Maybe by next season, both men will be around more often. Seeing them together makes me wonder whether he really needs me.

THE DIAMOND on my left ring finger catches the light refracting from the crystal chandelier in the home office as I search for the binder. I could have sworn I'd locked it in the bottom drawer, but it's not where I last remember seeing it. If he found it, he'd be smart enough to assemble the pieces that comprise the whole story. It was shortsighted of me to leave it anywhere he could potentially read it. If he knew what I had done—why I did what I did—it could mean the end of this new life of mine. Fraud is one of the circumstances that allow for an annulment rather than a divorce, and marrying for money is borderline. It's hard to argue one way or the other with how quickly we got married after meeting.

Liam was home all week resting from the concussion, giving him extra time at home while I wrapped up loose ends at the office or helped Helen with the Thanksgiving dinner preparations. I wanted to stay home and help, but Jack's niece ran into some issues that no one else had learned how to troubleshoot. I don't need the money from that job anymore, but I might if I can't figure out where this binder is. The only safety net I have to fall back on is my best friend's apartment.

I search every nook and cranny I can think of in the huge house, but I don't know the house as well as he does. There could be a bookcase hiding a secret room that I wouldn't ever find without his showing me. Either way, I've run out of places to look, and until I can figure out what happened, I can't run away. It's too big of a loose end to leave behind in this life that's felt like a fairytale. That binder could unravel any hope I have to rebuild myself again.

RULE #10

Know when it's time to show your hand

THIS STOMACH FLU is kicking my butt. Liam is concerned with how little I'm able to keep down without puking it back up, but I'm hesitant to go to the doctor until it's been a few days since I don't have a fever. Sometimes it's just a bug that lasts a day or two. Either way, I insist that he sleep in one of the guest beds so that I don't get him sick. He wouldn't let me move to one of the other bedrooms, and the team needs him to stay healthy now that he's out of concussion protocol.

When I don't feel better by day three, I make an appointment to see my doctor. Helen drives me to the doctor because her "mom superpowers" kicked in when Liam called her. He doesn't want me driving when I'm at risk of puking, and I agree with his decision on this. Going to the doctor by myself is never a fun experience. Fortunately, my doctor had a last-minute cancellation and could squeeze me in today.

The nurse calls me back to one of the rooms to test my vitals. She asks, "When was the date that you started your last period?"

I pull my phone out of my pocket to check the app that I use to track my periods. Then, I double-check today's date and the date I last input my cycle. The nurse is patiently waiting for my response, but I mentally go through the last six weeks in my head. Time has been a blur lately, but I could have sworn that I had my cycle as usual. Being on a birth control pill made the short bleeding like clockwork.

I tell her the date I have in my phone calendar, and she says, "Since you're sexually active, we'll do a pregnancy test." But I don't need to take a test to know what it's going to say. I'm not suffering from the symptoms of a stomach bug or flu. I had forgotten to take my birth control with me when I went with Liam to Germany, but I didn't think it would be a big deal since it was only a few days. He also used a condom to be extra safe. But I know my body well enough to know that it's not a virus causing my nausea.

The nurse hands me a cup and leads me to the bathroom, spouting off instructions I've heard from my gynecologist. It's procedure for the gynecologist to make sure you're not pregnant before any examinations such as Pap smears.

My doctor confirms my suspicions and hands me a list of prenatal vitamins and a pamphlet with suggestions that might help with the morning sickness. At the front desk, I schedule my ultrasound. Outwardly, I'm cool, calm, and collected, but inwardly, I'm a raging storm. I still haven't found my binder full of incriminating evidence. If Liam found it and read it, my marriage could be over. He hasn't been acting any differently, but he's been caught up with getting off the injury list and onto the field again. And now a baby is growing inside of me that will forever tie me to him whether he wants to stay married to me or not. With what's in that binder, Liam could even file for full custody of our child once he or she is born.

As much as I want to talk to someone about this, I can't tell Helen about the pregnancy before I tell Liam. He deserves to be the first person to hear the news whether he takes it as good news or not. I'm quiet as Helen drives me home, but she doesn't push me to tell her what's in my head. People tend to let you be when you're not feeling well.

I crawl into bed to ward off my exhaustion and tired

thoughts, waking up to the sound of Liam in the shower hours later. One glance at the clock confirms that he's home much earlier than he has been all week. The sickness has been my excuse the last few days, but I've been keeping him at arm's length while trying to sort through what I want and how I feel. Would it matter to him that I want him for the right reasons now even if that's not how this started? Shortly after I hear the shower turn off, I hear another faucet turn on. A streak of light illuminates the bed and silhouettes his tall, muscular frame.

"Odette, are you awake?" His voice is gentle in case I wasn't. "I started a bath for you." At that moment, I know he hasn't read the binder. If he had, he wouldn't be this thoughtful or caring.

I roll over so that I'm facing him and say, "You didn't have to do that, but I appreciate it."

"Was the doctor able to find something to help you feel better?" He asks as I slowly sit up in bed.

It only takes a few seconds for the nausea to resurface and quicken my pace to the bathroom. Liam is behind me a split second later, holding back my hair as the contents of my stomach empty into the toilet. I don't know how my body is supposed to get the nutrients it needs to grow the baby inside me when it can't keep any of it down. When my body lets me relax, he helps me undress and into the warm bath.

"Call for me when you're done," he says as he leaves a crack in the door to our bedroom. If I had to guess, he's on his tablet studying plays on tape for the next game. The Knights have only a few more games left in the regular season, and if they win this week, they'll clinch their division and spot in the playoffs. With everything on his plate, the last thing Liam needs to worry about is a baby we didn't plan for, but I don't know how I can keep this a secret with how bad the morning sickness is. At some point, I'm going to start showing.

I soak in the tub as my worries stick around. The warm water doesn't wash them away as I'd hoped. Not trusting myself with how sick and weak I've felt, I call for my husband in the next room. He pulls a towel out of his towel warmer and wraps me in the soft cocoon. His actions are more caring than sensual as he helps me dry my body and change into my pajamas. I brush my teeth for what feels like the umpteenth time before crawling back into the same bed I'd escaped from only an hour before.

"My dad put the old house up for sale," Liam says as nonchalantly as he would were he talking about the weather. This news is far from ordinary small talk.

"Does that mean what I think it means?" I ask him, careful not to jump to conclusions.

His face grows so bright that he deserves an Oscar for how well he's hidden his excitement until now. "My dad is moving to Kansas City. Actually, he should already be on his way to my mom's with the moving truck. My concussion seemed to have knocked some sense into him, and they've been talking about the logistics since that day. I also think Thanksgiving with us made him realize that he wants to live closer and be more involved in my life outside of coming to games."

"And he's still head over heels for his wife," I add with certainty.

"Almost as head over heels as I am for mine," Liam flirts. "I had to bribe my mom not to tell you earlier because I wanted you to hear the news from me. That woman drives a hard bargain."

"Do I want to know what you promised her in exchange for her silence?"

"In this case, ignorance is bliss." He cuddles me for the first time in days, somehow aware that my sickness isn't contagious even though I haven't shared my true diagnosis. Within minutes, he's lightly snoring.

The news of Dan and Helen Cartwright's reconciliation is how I procrastinate sharing the news growing in my womb. It's a decision of both avoidance and not wanting to upstage the joy he must feel that his parents are getting back together after so many years in different states. It's a selfish decision made for selfless reasons or vice versa.

❦

THE ADVANTAGE of knowing the cause of my nausea is being able to mitigate the worst of the symptoms. By the next evening, I feel closer to my old self including all the guilt that's weighed on me since I married Liam. I'm not expecting him home due to his calendar showing a planned dinner with Arthur, but his presence is unmistakable as I peruse the dinner options for something that won't trigger my morning sickness. I pull the last of the lasagna from the freezer and preheat the oven while Liam showers. I sit on the loveseat tapping out additional wedding tasks on my phone when Liam's scent garners my attention.

"How long are you going to wait to tell me what's going on with you?" Liam asks from his spot on the other side of the loveseat. His tone isn't angry or upset. He's curious, and I have to tread lightly because I don't know how much he's pieced together. I can't be sure of whether or not he found and read my binder. He's much more likely to have figured out that secret than that of the pregnancy.

"What do you mean?" I feign innocence and dodge the inquiry by responding to his question with one of my own. Avoidant behavior at its finest.

He takes a few moments to think of how he wants to respond. The silence is dangerous as it buys him more time to think through my actions and lack of communication. The two main things going on with me are at odds with each other and could obliterate what we've built over the past few months.

"Ever since my concussion, you've been keeping me at arm's length," he starts, and I know there's more coming. "At first, I thought you were giving me space to heal and recover

156

without any setbacks from doing too much, but you never quite returned to normal. I don't know if it's because you've been sick or feeling lost without a full-time job during the week. You haven't been communicating with me about any of it, so the best I can do is guess. It's like you're ready to run away."

"Maybe things would be easier if I did," I say quietly as the tears I've held at bay threaten to escape. "You have this incredible life that you've built because of the hard work and discipline required to play football at a professional level. I feel as if I haven't added anything to your life that you didn't already have. You've had your family supporting you at every game. Despite your reputation when it came to dating, people respected you because you leave it all out on the field."

Liam appears confused and hurt and all the things I imagined he would be while reading through all my rules and plans to marry for money. "I love football, but it's a physically hard sport to play. Of the small fraction of us who get the privilege to play at the professional level, some only get a few years before the injuries become too much for them to compete. When I look back on my life as an old man in a rocking chair, this time will be so brief compared to the time I spend with my wife and children. You've added to my life by giving me something to look forward to after the game both now and when I'm no longer on the field with the Knights. Odette, I love you and want to build that future with you."

His words hit like the cooling burn of peppermint. He closes the short distance between us to pull me close to him and wipe away my tears with the pads of his thumbs. He lifts my chin to look into his storming blue eyes.

"I don't deserve you." I barely hear my whisper, but he shakes his head at my claim. There's a hint of mischief in his eyes that doesn't match the seriousness of this conversation.

"Is this about how you married me for my money?"

It's as I suspected and feared, but it doesn't clear the

confusion in my mind. How long has he known, and why would he confess his love to me knowing the ugly truth behind why I'd given this a chance?

"How long have you known?" I muster enough courage to ask.

Liam chuckles as a grin spreads across his face. He's not angry or upset or pushing me away. His arms around me are as firm as they were moments ago. "I've known from the night we met. In my line of work, I have to be able to discern a woman's motives to talk to me. Most are hungry for fame and attracted to my looks. You were too level-headed to be after me for the fame. Even though your main goal was the money, I could tell that you were genuinely interested in me. I saw a woman who knows what she wants and is beautiful and cunning enough to get it, and I fit the bill. But I'm also a man who knows what he wants when he sees it, and I wanted you. You're not the only mastermind in this marriage. After a few hours, I knew I could spend a lifetime with you. I don't care if the money is what first drew you in because I know that's not why you're still here."

Shock and relief circulate through my body as I process his words. "I thought you had found out from my binder full of incriminating evidence."

"Oh, I did find that," he says with laughter. "I knew I was attracted to your brain, but I didn't know just how detailed your scheming was. You could put those skills to work as an assistant to the team's general manager. Anyway, I relocated your binder to my safe so that no one else accidentally stumbles upon it. Your gold-digger ways are our little secret."

"I still don't understand why you're so calm about this," I say while shaking my head.

His smile is soft as he reminds me, "I told you that I love you and want to build a future with you. Everyone has yellow flags and room for improvement, and that was something I was willing to tolerate and use to my advantage. Now, that we've come to an understanding on that, is there anything that you need to tell me?"

I calculate what the chances are that he might have stumbled across my prenatal vitamins in the few days I've had them. Given that he hasn't been home much since being cleared to practice again, it's less likely than it was that he would find the binder. This secret cannot stay hidden for long though.

"I wasn't sick with the flu or a stomach bug," I admit as a way to buy myself time or to build the suspense. Honestly, I'm not sure why I'm stalling. He stays silent, but his facial expression tells me to continue. "That was morning sickness because I'm pregnant."

"The only time we weren't careful were the few days in Germany—"

"That seems to be when it happened. Everything has been such a whirlwind after we got back that I lost track of the weeks. I didn't even notice the missed period or any of the other signs."

Before he can respond, the oven timer goes off. Liam gently pulls himself away to keep our dinner from burning. I move from the loveseat to a barstool at the kitchen island and watch as he throws together a salad for each of us. I can't decipher his mood until he looks up at me with a mischievous gleam in his eyes before he shakes his head and looks away again.

"I thought I was going to squeeze a confession of love out of you," he admits as he slides a plate in front of me. "I was not expecting news that I'm going to be a father. If it weren't obvious that you were as surprised as I am, I would congratulate you on outsmarting me in that respect. I need you to be honest with me though. Are you still here because you love me or are you here because you're pregnant and don't want to end up in the same cycle as your mother?"

His question hits a nerve. My mother is the whole reason behind how I've ended up in this position with a professional athlete as my husband and the father of my growing baby. She wanted me to have the life she never had because she saw marriage as a means of gaining money for security. While I know she loves me, she didn't teach me the value of love in a marriage. She didn't teach me how and when to let my walls down with someone who had proven himself trustworthy of my heart. My mother couldn't teach me what she didn't know. Staying here for love goes against the instincts I spent a lifetime honing.

I look at the looming figure of the Kansas City Knights' star tight end, remembering the moments between his hit on the field and being by his side at the hospital. I wouldn't have entertained the idea of leaving if I wasn't scared of how much I've fallen in love with him since the night of our rushed wedding. Pregnancy or not, I don't think I would have gathered enough courage to follow through on that fear of attachment.

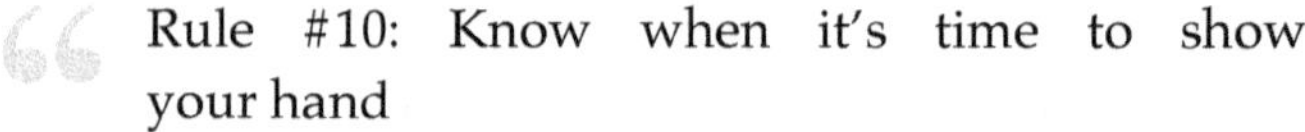

Rule #10: Know when it's time to show your hand

"I'm here because I love you," I say with a smile and tears in my eyes. As swiftly as if he were on the field, he rounds the kitchen island to pull me into a kiss filled with a lifetime of promises. It feels like a godsend that we already planned a wedding because I suddenly want to marry this man all over again for real.

"If I weren't so hungry right now, I would skip dinner," Liam says with exasperation. "We both need to eat. We also need to figure out how we're going to tell my parents that they have a grandchild on the way before we can add all your appointments and the due date to my calendar since my assistant has access to that. I don't want to ruin the surprise—"

I interrupt, "One thing at a time. You have practice tomorrow, remember. I'll brainstorm and come up with a few ideas that we can go over tomorrow. Christmas is so close, we could just stick something in a box and put their names on it. My mom will be here, too."

He takes a deep breath to calm himself before he sits in the chair beside me at the kitchen island. After he chews and swallows a few bites of his salad, he asks, "How are you doing with the morning sickness? You seem to be better than you were, but I want to be sure."

"I am feeling a lot better," I say between bites. "I scheduled the first ultrasound for a time that shouldn't conflict with your practices, training, or games. I assumed that no matter how the conversation went, you would want to be there."

"You assumed correctly on that," he confirms. "I'm relieved to know that even when you had doubts, you knew I wouldn't be like your father. I want a family, specifically with you, and I'm ready for that family. Write down the details so that I have the information somewhere that isn't accessible to my assistant."

I wait until I'm finished with my dinner to grab a notepad and pen for jotting down the appointment details. Liam cleans up our dishes from dinner before he scoops me into his arms bridal-style and carries me to our bedroom.

"I'm going to need you to repeat your confession of undying love for me a few more times to make up for lost time," he whispers in my ear an hour later before falling asleep.

THE HOLIDAYS ARE busy for normal people, but they're insane in the world of professional football. Helen shows up to games in Knights Christmas sweaters and a wedding band on her left hand again. Dan never took his ring off during the time his wife lived in a different state. The fans hardly notice the personal lives of their favorite players amid the string of surprising losses for the Knights. My mom flew into town two days before Christmas to stay for a week because Liam had to play against a division rival at noon on Christmas Day. We celebrated on Christmas Eve as Liam and I shared the news of the baby with ultrasound photos to pass around. Sasha has been on high alert on social media for any posts suggesting that I might be pregnant. Instead, they're all focused on the uncharacteristic turnovers of Arthur as the team defeated themselves.

While December football wasn't kind to the Knights, they snagged the third seed in their conference, guaranteeing at least one home game during the wildcard round. By the time all the seeds are in place, the team faces one of the toughest routes to make it to the league championship game. Their first game—the one with home-field advantage—is against the Seagulls. Had their matchup earlier in the season been on American soil, it would have been at Camelot Stadium. Instead, Martin Mound's first game against the Knights in Kansas City is higher stakes. To add to the storyline, the weather forecast is predicting lows that would make this game one of the coldest in league history.

"Games like this are when the true fans show up," Helen mutters on our walk from her car to the stadium. The meteorologists weren't exaggerating when they predicted arctic blasts. The wind chill will make this night unbearable and possibly dangerous for anyone who shows up unprepared. The concessions are preparing hot chocolate stations while emergency services ready themselves for the frostbite cases that are inevitable when fans are drinking too much.

"Historically, the Seagulls do not fare well in cold-weather games," Dan says as we watch the teams warm up on the field. The field at Camelot Stadium has heaters underneath and benches that are heated. The Knights have gone through many winter games in their open-air stadium, but the Seagulls have no way to prepare for this extreme in their city of beaches and palm trees.

"There are reels on social media from fans showing beers freezing within seconds," Natalie says as she shakes her head at the absurdity. "In this one, the water bottles are freezing after they're taken out of the fridge. The fridge is keeping them warm. Why did I let you convince me to come tonight?"

"Because we're in a climate-controlled suite," I respond with a shrug. "And you can warm up your car using an app on your phone. We're hardly braving the elements when compared to the players and fans."

While not an overly exciting game due to the defensive dominance, the Knights won as many suspected they would. What I wasn't prepared for was how little alone time I would have with my husband once the playoffs were in full swing. Liam was either at practice, watching footage, or sleeping. The players didn't watch or listen to the sports commentators throughout the week, but they were all aware of the doubts circling through the air. Arthur had never played a post-season match outside of Camelot until now, and their next opponent had beaten them in Kansas City in December during the regular season. In recent years, the Elks have been consistent contenders in the playoff picture.

Due to the lake effect, this part of New York State always has a layer of snow in the winter. Compared to last weekend in Kansas City, the temperatures here are warmer, even if the air is still below freezing. The fans of the Elks are accustomed to braving the winter weather to cheer for their favorite team. Many of them help shovel the stadium to prepare for what they're hoping is a step closer to the league championship game. The Knights walk onto the field as the underdogs in the divisional round.

Sasha, Dan, Helen, and I are bundled up in a guest suite with Jen and her kids as the players warm up on the field. Half an hour before kickoff, Lance joins us after braving the snow-dusted roads for nearly seven hours. I would ask why he didn't hop on a nonstop flight from Boston, but he looks worn out from the trek. I'm sure Helen and Dan already gave him the easier option.

While the Elks fans cleared out most of the snow, there is enough of it left to form the snowballs flying toward Arthur and Liam when they emerge onto the field. The atmosphere is loud with the boos of the New Yorkers, but enough Knights fans showed up to put a dent in the home-field advantage.

"You're not drinking tonight, Lance?" Jen asks my brother-in-law as he sips a cup of coffee. A few years ago when the Knights won the league championship, a much younger Lance showed up to one of the playoff games in Liam's suite with a few of his fraternity brothers as his guests. During the first part of the game, they drank to lessen the blow of the Knights being down by more than two touchdowns. The team managed to come back and win, and a very drunk and shirtless Lance was broadcast across the sports channels. Though Helen was also in the suite with him, not even his mother could stop him from celebrating the improbable win.

"A smart man only makes that mistake once," Lance says with a twinkle in his eyes as if whether he would ever do it again is still to be determined. Tonight, though, is not the night.

The game is as electric as anticipated, a duel that continues to deliver some of the best football of this generation. Even Sasha spends more time looking at the field than at her phone. It feels as if something game-changing might happen if I glance away for even a second. I'm thankful that the morning sickness subsided in time for the playoffs, but my bladder doesn't hold for quite as long as it used to. At the end of every quarter, I take advantage of the restrooms. I bump into Jen on my way back to my seat during halftime.

"How far along are you?" She whispers the question even though our surroundings are too loud for anyone else to overhear.

"About nine or ten weeks, I think," I say to her as I try to do the mental math in my head. Time has been flying by so quickly since the playoffs began that it's hard to keep track of what day it is. So far, I've done well to disguise the growing baby bump.

Jen glances at her children who are playing with Dan and Helen before returning her attention to me. "They must be over the moon about a grandchild on the way. It definitely sweetens the deal for Dan finally moving to be closer. I know he didn't always come off this way to the public, but Liam is very family-oriented. Finding you and getting more time with Dan has really settled him in a way that's making him a better player than he was before. A lot of those men on the field can do what they do because they have the support of their families behind the scenes. I wish more fans realized that."

"I think they're starting to with social media giving them an inside look at what it's like to parent while being successful in professional sports," I say to encourage her. Motherhood has made Jen more relatable to fans than she was before she had kids. The players on the team who manage to stay out of legal trouble in the off-season are the ones who pour their energy into their families.

The nerves and adrenaline of the second half are so high that part of me wants the game to end so I can finally relax and know the outcome. It continues to be a close game. The Knights are up by three points near the end, but I'm almost certain that we're going to have to sit through overtime as the Elks have the ball close enough to kick a field goal to tie the game. What we weren't expecting is for the kick to be wide to the right as the Knights advance to the conference championship match. The only thing standing between Arthur and another chance at a league championship win is the top seed of the conference.

Playoff games draw a larger audience than the usual regular season game because it's the only professional football game airing at that time. The influx of comments keeps Sasha glued to her phone more than she usually is. Fans obsess over the matching outfits that Arthur and Jen's kids wore to the game almost as much as they comment on the photo of Liam lifting me into the air for a kiss when I ran onto the field at the end of the game. My diamond ring sparkles under the lights.

"This makes me believe in love," reads one near the top. Me too, kid. Me too.

THE NARRATIVE ON the sports channels has the Knights on edge. This team knows how to win in these environments, but they're aware that the Crows earned the top seed in the play-offs for a reason. Their quarterback is equally as talented as Arthur, though with a slightly different skill set. In the other conference, the teams battling for a league championship game appearance are the team that lost to the Knights a few years ago and a team that hasn't ever been to the league championship game. The outcome of these games could determine dynasties.

Even on the plane ride to Baltimore, Liam and Arthur pour over film and plays. All week, Liam has been inspecting the Crows' defense for soft spots and weaknesses. Studying can only prepare them so much for the real thing because each team makes adjustments depending on their opponents.

"How are you feeling about the game?" I ask Liam the night before as we settle into bed.

"When I was first drafted by the Knights, they were good, but they weren't yet at this championship-caliber level," he says as he sifts through the memories of his first few seasons. "Back then, every playoff game was a gift. Once we drafted Arthur and he stepped up to the starting quarterback posi-tion, that aspect didn't change. We've played in every confer-ence championship game for the last six seasons, and this is the first time we won't have home-field advantage. Beyond the regular season, whether the team is at its best or its worst, every postseason game is a gift because it's never guaranteed."

"That makes sense," I say as I mindlessly caress his arm.

He smiles and looks at me, "It's almost as big of a blessing as having you and our baby. This season is different because I have you out there cheering me on. Once the dust settles and we're past the playoffs and the wedding, I think I'd like to get back to church on Sundays. What are your thoughts on that?"

My mind flashes back to the moments when I prayed that my husband would be safe and healthy after his hit on the field. My grandparents took me to church a few times when I was younger, but I don't remember much from those experiences apart from the happy adults. Their beliefs never really stuck with my mom, but maybe she would have been less closed off had she had someone she could believe in. "If God is the one who's kept you safe and strong in this sport, I'm open to getting to know Him."

THE KNIGHTS' defense and offense both show up strong in the first quarter of the game. Arthur and Liam are in sync as Liam makes an improbable catch in the end zone, giving the Knights the first touchdown and score of the game. The Crows are quick to tie the game in the next drive as the stadium erupts in cheers for the home team. Helen grabs my hand and gives it a reassuring squeeze. This is only the beginning.

Arthur scrambles on the field as the Crows' defense tries to stop the momentum of the Knights. I'm holding my breath as our quarterback releases another throw that my husband somehow snags and secures while surrounded by the opposing team. When they replay it in slow motion, I know that's a catch that will be in the highlight reels. That's a catch that guarantees his spot in the Hall of Fame. Their second drive results in another touchdown.

Even when our defense takes the field, we can't look away. Sasha is paying closer attention to the field than to her phone. It's like we know before it happens. One of the players forces a fumble out of the hands of the Crows quarterback, and another Knights player retrieves the ball to ensure the turnover. America has been waiting all season for this kind of football game. Though our offense is stopped short of a third touchdown, our placekicker scores on the field goal to put us ten points ahead.

After a hot start to the game on both sides, the defense for both teams holds the scoreboard steady. The momentum swings again when the Knights force and recover another fumble in the end zone, resulting in a touchback. What would have been a touchdown for the Crows turns into a no-score and automatic ball in the hands of Arthur. The Crows' next attempt to score is an interception in the end zone.

"I'm baking pies for that defense of ours," Helen says with a wide smile.

On the drive that could solidify our spot in the league championship game, Arthur takes a chance and throws a long shot at one of the receivers who struggled with drop passes during the regular season. Like the rest of the team, he steps up to the challenge and makes a catch to guarantee that his football career isn't over yet. In the suite, we jump from our seats in exuberant celebration as the players on the sideline do the same. Though they're the minority in the audience, the Knights fans make their presence known. To the Crows, we're the villains in this story, but from our vantage point, Arthur is the hero establishing a dynasty.

THE NIGHT I married Liam Cartwright had many of the same elements as the spontaneous weddings that take place in Vegas. Little did I know that saying yes to that man would mean going to Las Vegas as a VIP guest at the football game of football games. The Sphere features an advertisement of Arthur specifically filmed for the round display as the football circles back to him. The stadium hosting the championship has been home to the Knights' biggest and longest rival for the last few years. Now, we're the designated home team on this field where the team plays at least once a season due to being in the same division.

"Have you heard the rumors about the Knights flag buried underneath the stadium during construction?" Liam asks as we walk hand in hand to the event for press coverage. Sasha and Natalie specifically chose outfits for me that would disguise my small baby bump, including the loose Liam Cartwright jersey that I'm wearing tonight.

"You mean the one that they revealed was just a rumor?" I ask as the noise of crowds increases.

Liam gives me a skeptical expression as he says, "That's what they want everyone in Vegas to believe so that they don't go digging around for it. Someone already claimed to have dug it up, but the location would have been nearly impossible to get to during construction. You can't easily dig up concrete like that once it's cured. My gut says it's still down there."

"Your gut also says that you think we're having a boy, but as the one carrying this child, I think our firstborn will be a girl." I make sure no one is around as I tease him. The plan is to keep the pregnancy under wraps for as long as possible, especially during this week with all eyes on the Knights.

Sasha finds us before Liam can give his rebuttal, shifting our focus to the wide array of questions we can expect from the press tonight. We might be here to talk about the biggest game in professional football, but someone is likely to bring up the upcoming wedding and pregnancy rumors. After years of fielding questions from reporters, Liam is a natural in the spotlight. One of the reasons he married me is that I'm quick on my feet in unfamiliar situations. I may not be able to give weight to my mother's relationship advice these days, but she did instill in me a useful skill set for my role.

Neither of us is prepared for the final question of the night. "Liam and Odette, do either of you have anything to comment on the rumors that there are records of a marriage license with both your names dated back in August?"

By the look on Sasha's and Helen's faces, neither of them was anticipating the question. I squeeze Liam's hand both in reassurance and to urge him to answer the question however he sees fit. Of all of us, he's the one who wanted to be honest and forthcoming in the beginning about our relationship.

"I'm just surprised that it's taken my fans this long to uncover our secret," Liam says with his signature smile to lighten the mood. I plaster a smile on my face to match his as I wait to see what else he has up his sleeve. "One of my best talents on the field is seeing an opportunity and capitalizing on it. Not only has that ability helped the Knights win when it matters most, but it's also helped me make wise investments. When I met Odette, I knew right away that a future with her was one of those life-changing opportunities."

Before we can retreat through the tunnel and toward the locker room, another reporter raises his hand and light-heartedly asks, "Next time—like when there's a Baby Cartwright—can you let us know before showing up to a game with a baby?"

Liam winks at the reporter before he leads me away from the public eye.

"As if I could hide this bump long enough for that," I mutter.

I'M USED to being around wealthy people, and I'm used to being around the football culture. What I'm not acclimated to is how those two worlds merge at the league championship games. There are fans from both teams present in the audience, especially since the Knights' opponent is from San Francisco. Some people are here to be seen or noticed, without any care as to how the game ends or how Usher's performance during halftime will compare to past shows.

"Seeing this reminds me that even though Liam is an athlete, he's considered an entertainer by some," Helen says as she scans the crowds.

"It's even worse because we're in Vegas," Sasha reminds her as she sits down in the open chair to my left. Jen sits on the other side of Helen with a few of the other players' wives and girlfriends occupying the other seats. Given the celebrities in attendance tonight, we would have been without the plexiglass separating us from the crowds, but the clips of Liam's confession from the press conference have been circulating like wildfire. Plus, we're playing in the city of one of our biggest rivals. Liam and his teammates pitched in to get a suite for all of us to watch the game together.

I can't pinpoint when it all sinks in. It might be when Reba McEntire sings the National Anthem or when Matt kicks the ball across the field for the other team to receive. Or, it could be when my phone vibrates with a text from my mom sending me a photo of her view of the game at a sports bar her new boyfriend frequents. I might not be able to go to my mom for reliable relationship advice, but I can be a model to her of what a healthy relationship with secure attachment looks like.

When it looks like the Miners are likely to score on the first drive of the game, their star running back fumbles the football. The Knights' defense recovers the ball as Arthur, Liam, and the rest of the offense prepare to take the field for the first time in this high-stakes game. In this duel of the best of the best, the Knights are unable to get the ball moving down the field. The teams go back and forth as the defense on both sides holds their ground and forces the ball to be punted. The first quarter of the championship game ends with neither team scoring.

"I would rather the game be scoreless and tied than be down by ten points," Helen says as she gives me a reassuring smile. She and I might share that sentiment, but I know that Liam is on the sideline chomping at the bit to get back out there and gain some momentum. The Miners score a field goal early in the second quarter by setting the record for the longest field goal in the league championship game.

As the Knights' offense neared the end zone, one of our young running backs fumbles the ball, which is recovered by the Miners. Due to the excellence of the defense, the punters for both teams are getting more work in than they likely have in any other game this season. The Miners break the monotony by scoring a touchdown and an extra point with less than five minutes remaining in the first half. Arthur and the Knights take advantage of the game clock and score a field goal to close the second quarter, lessening the lead of their opponent.

"The Miners are only winning by one score," Dan reminds us to try to lift the atmosphere of our box. "Seven points is nothing in this game, especially when Arthur is running on all cylinders. He's proven that he knows how to come back from behind when it matters the most. Plus, the Knights are receiving the ball in the second half."

On the field below, workers are a well-organized machine as they set the stage for Usher's halftime show. The entertainment isn't enough to placate the nerves I feel on behalf of my husband and the team, but Jen and I both sing and dance to the music that frequented our playlists growing up. At the end of the halftime show, my phone vibrates with a text from my mother.

MOM

You're the only reason I knew any of those songs. Congratulations on being old enough that you're the main audience

> I didn't realize how old he is until I looked it
> up. The choreography on skates is even
> more impressive now

Despite the two children clinging to her, Jen reaches across to hold mine and Helen's hands in her own, squeezing them before letting go.

"They've been here before, and they know what to do," she reminds us as the teams return to the field from the locker room. "They were behind by this much at halftime during last year's championship, and look how that one turned out."

Jen's speech is for herself as much as it is for the rest of us in the suite. When the Knights offense takes the field, they fumble and recover their ball, losing yards in the process. To get out of the bind they're in on third down, Arthur throws an interception for the first time in this postseason. Our suite is silent enough that you could hear a pin drop. Despite the mishap, the Miners are unable to convert the interception into points on the board.

The momentum shifts slightly when Arthur makes a connection with Liam on the field. Though the drive is stopped short, the Knights have one of the best placekickers in the league. His record is longer than the distance he faces now, and his accuracy and power behind the kick earn the Knights another three points to lessen the Miners' lead. It also beats the record for the longest field goal in the league championship game from earlier in this showdown.

The teams continue to punt the ball, hoping for another spark of momentum. Special teams is on full display when the Knights recover a muffed punt that hit the foot of a Miners player. In one play, Arthur capitalizes on the opportunity by throwing his first touchdown pass of the game. It took nearly three full quarters, but the Knights have the lead for the first time tonight.

The Miners respond with a touchdown of their own, but their extra point kick is blocked by one of the Knights' linebackers on special teams. That missed point is what allows the Knights to tie the game with a field goal. As we watch on the edge of our seats, both teams score a field goal each before the clock winds down. With the score tied, the championship is going into overtime.

A few years ago, the league tweaked the overtime rules for postseason games to guarantee that both teams would have an opportunity to possess the ball. I've heard countless conversations between Arthur and Liam about strategies for the rule change, including what to do if we win the coin flip. The Miners win the coin flip, but they choose to receive the ball first. Whether they realize it or not, they've chosen to let Arthur have the last say in this game. This is exactly how the Knights have planned to win.

The new overtime rules turn out to be irrelevant because our defense forces the Miners to settle for a field goal. Nearly everyone in our suite holds their breaths as we watch Arthur rush with the ball to convert on a fourth down. We're witnessing the best part of football as the Knights continue to progress into the red zone. Our nerves are at an all-time high every time the ball is hiked to start the play.

"This is the play that wins it," I say as I watch my husband and his teammates line up at the third-yard line. I don't know how I knew, but the next play is the one that will be shown in multiple highlight reels for years. When the receiver catches the perfect pass from Arthur, the stadium erupts with noise and confetti. Back-to-back league championship winners. We all make a beeline for the suite exit to run onto the field and find our champions.

Security helps guide and escort us onto the field. Strips of red and gray confetti fall like snowflakes around me as Liam scoops me into his arms. He has a sheen of sweat and the glow of ecstasy on his face as he kisses me as if his next breath depends on it.

"Winning is better with you here," he says into the crook of my neck before he sets me down on my feet. "Everything is better with you here."

EPILOGUE

After you break all the rules

Transatlantic flights are one thing; transatlantic flights while pregnant are a different level of uncomfortable. It's only the second trimester, but I'm ready to no longer be pregnant. At this point, I'm still hiding the small bump well. With the championship game and parade behind us, we're not in the spotlight in the same way we were during the regular season and the playoffs. By the time the next season starts, I'll be handing my firstborn to my mom for a few hours while watching my husband play the sport he loves.

"How are you feeling?" Liam asks me as I return to our first-class seats after going to the bathroom.

"A lot better since the nausea subsided a few weeks ago," I reply. "If you want twelve of these, be prepared to adopt."

Liam laughs at the inside joke. "One day at a time and one child at a time as long as all of them are with you. That's my only requirement for the future. Actually, no. I'm also good with twins or triplets or however many could come from a single pregnancy."

"Real smooth," I say with a smile. "I knew what you meant. I'm not sure if you noticed, but we're on a plane en route to Venice because we're renewing our vows in a week. You're stuck with me and this baby."

I notice when his expression shifts before he asks, "Your dad is still coming to the wedding, right? I know he hasn't been around much, but he seemed appreciative that you extended an olive branch when we met him."

My father's legacy in the sports world landed him in the stands at the championship game where Liam's play suggestion resulted in the final touchdown that won the game. Retired basketball star Percy Donovan was among the athletes and celebrities who gathered to congratulate the team. He used the opportunity to apologize to me for all the ways he wasn't around. It wasn't for show or the media, and I knew that he was sincere in his request to be part of my life in whatever capacity I would allow. I suspect he's on speaking terms with my mom again, but I'm waiting for her to bring it up.

"His flight from Seattle should be landing around the same time as ours," I say. Most of our close friends and family are flying to Venice today and tomorrow. Some are on this same flight with us. There are enough of us that Liam arranged for a private boat to take us around while we're there.

Liam looks at our surroundings before he whispers, "I think Dan and Helen are planning to elope while we're on our honeymoon. I mean, they're technically still married, but you know what I mean. Mom doesn't want to plan a whole ceremony and reception to renew their vows because helping with ours is enough for her. Now I see where I got it from."

"At least they're eloping in Europe. It's a bit more romantic than Kansas City, as beautiful as it can be at times," I tease him loud enough for his parents to overhear. Anyone in our cabin who isn't part of the celebration will likely be annoyed by the end of this trek.

"I'm pulling for the countryside in France," Helen says as she shoots a mischievous grin towards Dan. "This one would rather stay in Paris among the hustle and bustle of the city."

Dan playfully throws up his hands as he says, "You know

what? I don't care where we go, as long as we go together. I'm not letting my stubbornness stall our life together any longer."

"That is why I'm still single," Lance says as he shakes his head with a smile. He elaborates further, "I haven't found anyone yet that I feel that way about. Maybe I'll find her in Minneapolis. Better yet, maybe she's in Italy." He waggles his eyebrows, eliciting an eye-roll from his mother.

Helen changes the subject, "When are you two going to tell us the gender of our first grandchild?"

Even though Liam and I opted for the blood test to find out the gender, we've kept the results to ourselves to avoid it overshadowing the wedding. What they don't know is that the streamers for the send-off are also serving as our gender reveal. I give Helen the same expression I have the other times she's inquired about the gender.

"You'll know sooner rather than later," Liam hints without spoiling the surprise.

ONCE WE LAND at the Venice Marco Polo Airport, everything is a whirlwind. Our private boat waits for us to embark with our luggage as Liam carries both our suitcases, despite my insistence that I'm capable of rolling my own. With the number of professional football players who are in our party, none of them are going to let me lift anything heavy while we're here.

To give the experience a more authentic feel, Liam and I decide to stay in separate rooms until the wedding. He carries my suitcase to the front door of the suite I'm sharing with Natalie when she arrives in a few hours. Then, he disappears into the suite he's sharing with Lance. Between jet lag and pregnancy, the only thing on my mind is a short nap to re-energize.

"Odette, you know better than to sleep this early in the day," Natalie's voice says as my eyes drift open. My best friend is standing a few feet away with her suitcase next to mine. "The best way to adjust to the time difference is—"

"To push through until bedtime," I interrupt her as I sit up. "I'm pregnant though. I need a nap if I'm going to get through a rehearsal and seven-course dinner with that many people." It's an excuse to cover up the fact that I forgot to set an alarm. I had wanted to explore the resort and make a plan of how to use the few pockets of free time that I had, but the bride wasn't allowed to be late for her rehearsal dinner.

Natalie unzips her suitcase and sorts through her clothes before pulling out a green dress with the tag dangling from it. She would bring a dress that hasn't been worn or washed yet. "Are you showering before or after dinner? I take whichever one you don't want."

"After," I say even though I suspect I'll regret that choice when the time comes. Natalie helps me get dressed and do my makeup to hide the evidence of both my nap and lingering sleepiness.

"I should text Liam and Lance to make sure they both didn't pass out the same way I did," I say as Natalie touches up her makeup. I don't know what she has to touch up since the girl likely looked ready for a runway when her international flight landed. My screen has several text notifications from Liam who managed to tour the grounds like I wanted to. The string of messages includes photos as his way of including me.

Natalie pauses with a pensive expression on her face. "Have I met Lance yet?"

"Yes, you have both been in the same suite at Camelot to watch a Knights game," I reply, remembering when Liam was still out recovering from his concussion. "You've probably crossed paths a dozen times by now just throughout the last few months."

Natalie shrugs as she finishes in the mirror. Together, we walk to the dining room, the roar of laughter unmistakable as we near the crowd of our wedding party and guests. Liam is already standing near the table and catches my eye as we walk in. You'd think he hadn't seen me in days with the way he smolders as he checks out my dress. With the way Lance and Natalie look at each other, you'd think they were meeting for the first time. I'm certain they've at least been in the same room before tonight though.

From my seat, I watch Coach Anderson as his eyes drink in the array of Italian delicacies on display. His wife lightly slaps his hand when he reaches for one of the antipasti. I don't know who thought it was a wise idea to put food out before we were finished going over the order of events. It's time to speed through this rehearsal so that we can all enjoy the remainder of the evening. Because all of us are ready to eat more than we can stomach, the rehearsal is quick and easy.

"Lance and Natalie?" Liam whispers to me as the waiters serve the salad course. Like him, I'm also trying to figure out if the chemistry between my brother-in-law and best friend is strong enough to last after this destination wedding.

"You married me on the night we met, so nothing is off the table with those two," I joke as I scan the crowd around us. Everyone that I could want in attendance is here with us, including my father. He's making an effort, which isn't too hard considering the sports world is his comfort zone. Some athletes go as far as to play in more than one professional sports league, juggling the practices and game responsibilities. Then again, being a good father like Arthur is its own type of professional sport.

Liam shows me around the resort as the sun sinks below the horizon accented by lagoon waves. Under the haze of dusk with lights reflecting off the water, I can see why Sasha insisted on going all out on the private island resort. Venice has a plethora of beautiful wedding venue options from cathedrals to terraces, but this part is secluded from the American tourists who would recognize Liam and Arthur. Depending on the football fan, some would even recognize me due to the media attention.

"What kind of masochist agrees to sleep in a separate room from his hot wife in a romantic setting like this?" Liam asks as we near our rooms for the night.

I raise my eyebrows as I reply, "The masochist who suggested this idea is the same masochist who plays a professional sport where grown men wear tight pants and tackle each other regularly. He mentioned something about going all in on the experience of a wedding."

"It's all or nothing in both situations. To be fair, I'm tall enough to need all my clothes tailored. Gotta pay for that somehow, and football in America pays well. Plus, I now have a very beautiful and pregnant freeloader to pay for." His teasing smile makes me want to stall saying goodnight, but exhaustion is winning this round of tug-o-war. His kiss is sweet before we go our separate ways.

KNOWING that we're already married—that neither of us regrets the decision to marry on a whim—makes the wedding day less nerve-wracking. There's no trace of cold feet or runaway bride. Two mothers are doing their best to hold back their tears as we wait for the ceremony to begin. I can understand why Helen is misty-eyed, but my mother doesn't wear her heart on her sleeve.

"I would have understood if you had asked your father to walk you down the aisle," she says to me once we have a moment alone. "It's the tradition of it."

Staring into my mother's eyes, I say, "He's not the one who was in my life to have any say in giving me away. Even though I spent part of my childhood in boarding school, you were still the one making sure I was always taken care of in the best way you knew how." God knows the woman was far from a perfect mother, but she was still a mother in her imperfect way. I would rather have an imperfect mom than none at all.

The coordinator directs the wedding party on how to line up and where to walk. Liam and his groomsmen are at the altar, watching as each piece falls into place. The man at the other end of the aisle is the only one I see as I walk toward him in the wedding dress that barely hides my baby bump. I can't imagine doing this with anyone else.

We recite the same vows, this time knowing and loving the person we're making these promises to. He's more than a man with millions in the bank and three league championship wins under his belt. Liam Cartwright is a man who loves his family and backs up his words with actions. Even though I already have his last name, there's something about the officiant's announcement that makes it more real than before. I'm not pretending to be someone I'm not as he kisses me in a way that reminds me of the first time his lips touched mine.

As we join our closest friends and family at the reception, I'm reminded of why we went through the hassle of all the planning for this day. I spent years focused on how to marry a gold mine and not enough time imagining what it would feel like to celebrate that marriage. Liam might be used to crowds of people fixing their attention on him, but I'm still growing used to sharing his spotlight. He kisses my hand before we sit at the head table between Natalie and Lance. I might have to convince Lance to try living in Kansas City rather than Minneapolis if my suspicions are correct.

Due to the lack of nerves, I have no issues eating the food served at my wedding, savoring the Italian seafood that Liam opted to splurge on. The final bill for this wedding would shock most people, even without the price of international flights. When Sasha had gone over the menu quote with me and Liam, he said, "I want to make sure that this wedding costs more than Arthur and Jen's just so I can one-up him on something."

My father walks over to our table to congratulate us, and Liam stands to shake his hand. Jokingly, the man who was absent from my life until a few weeks ago says, "If I'd been around like I should have, I might have steered you away from professional athletes. It worked out though because I think you've snagged one of the good ones." He ends his statement with a wink before heading back to his table.

Arthur is the first to give a toast, sharing embarrassing stories about Liam. "Last year, he didn't even try to find a date and brought his mom to the gala instead. She was a lot more fun to be around than any of his other last-minute dates. I was there the night that he met Odette, but I wasn't expecting him to tell me that he married her. I mean, that's one way to prove you're not afraid of commitment. All joking aside, she was a good choice, and I'm glad that I got to be here to help celebrate this win that goes beyond a football season."

Lance has his own tales to tell of their shenanigans growing up, including the many ways Liam tried to impress girls in high school.

"If I didn't know any better, I would think this was a roast instead of a toast," I tease Liam as Lance hands the mic to Natalie.

When the applause quiets down, she says, "Just let the record show that I'm the one who dragged her out that night for her birthday. I take full responsibility for how this ended, and I expect to be the godmother of that baby you're having." Between Natalie and Liam, this child is going to be spoiled.

Once the cake is cut and the dance floor opens up, time flies. Liam dances like this is the touchdown dance he's been practicing all week, showing up his other groomsmen. Dan and Helen join in with moves that prove the talent is genetic. Natalie even manages to drag a hesitant Lance onto the floor when the typical group dance songs play through the speakers.

"We're making those two the godparents for our kids, right?" I ask Liam as I watch the obvious flirting between my best friend and brother-in-law. I still haven't figured out how they didn't notice each other before this weekend.

One glance at the clock tells me that it's almost time for the send-off. Noticing the same, Liam squeezes my hand in reassurance. The only other person who knows about this gender reveal is Sasha, and she's at the exit with her phone camera ready to capture the moment. Our guests line up around the designated aisle with their streamer poppers in hand, ready to shower us with bursts of color.

"Three," I begin to count down.

"Two," he says.

"One," we say together as we rush through the cloud of pink streamers that cascade between us and our wedding night.

Before we make our escape, Liam turns around and unfurls a flag that says, "It's a girl" just long enough for everyone to read it. Even as the voices begin to fade, I can hear Helen's excitement over having a girl in the family.

"Did I mention that all my cousins are also boys?" Liam asks as he shakes his head at her excitement. "This will be the first Cartwright girl born into the family in the last few decades."

With a mischievous expression on my face, I say, "Sounds like I'll have to teach her everything I know about how to marry someone wealthy. With the way you and your family are about to spoil her, she won't know how to live a middle-class lifestyle. My mom and I can start the trophy wife training as soon as she's old enough to talk."

"Babe, you're not a trophy wife," Liam says as he scoops me into his arms to carry me over the threshold. "You're a stay-at-home mom who's about to take over planning all the events and endorsements for my charity. You might have initially married me for my money, but this is beyond that now. Trophy wives are only there for the benefits. Odette, you're a mastermind who fell in love and let herself open up to her own feelings. I'm the real gold digger for seeing your heart and marrying you for it."

IT WAS MY IDEA FIRST

In 2017, I spent much of my free time reading stories on the Episode app. I was fascinated with the idea of writing/coding my own story and jumped at the opportunity when they were having a themed contest. The story requirement was that it had to be about a dream job. I chose an unorthodox idea and essentially plotted a short story featuring a gold digger whose dream is to be a trophy wife. Because the draw of Episode is being able to choose your own path, that version has a love triangle.

On October 21, 2022, I listened to Taylor Swift's new Midnights album as "Mastermind" played in my car stereo. I could picture the scene in my head where the guy knows all along what her intentions are and thought it would make a great book. Then, I remembered that I had written that as a short story years before. I had also been thinking that a football story was a potential project after I finished what is now my book "At Second Sight." That story had to be written first, but then I would be free to rewrite my old story as a full novel with football added to the plot and Kansas City has the location.

I discussed the idea with my writing group well before I started drafting, and they helped me decide to use a tight end rather than a quarterback. I waited until November of 2023 to write, but by then, the unpredictable had occurred. Travis Kelce, who served as some of the inspiration for Liam, had started dating Taylor Swift, the artist behind the song that sparked the idea behind doing this as a novel. I was at the first Chiefs game where she made an appearance.

As I tend to in November, I wrote over 50,000 words of this book in November and then struggled to finish it as I switched gears to edit and publish "At Second Sight." Following that, I juggled multiple new life changes and went through life-altering health issues. Despite that, I knew that I had to get this out in the early part of football season for a fall release.

Firstly, I thank God for helping me get this out and giving me little nudges to remind me to work on this. It was a stretch for me to write these characters, and I didn't realize until I was almost done how much I unintentionally touched on her attachment style. It's one of those things that I learned about in the months I was writing the last few thousand words.

Thank you to my writing accountability group. Rachel, your excitement about this project was a constant reminder that this was worth putting out there. Erica, you're a great asset to us writers, and I hope to see your name on the front cover of a book soon. Esther, we all need that friend who begs for advanced copies. Danny, I found you by accident on Fiverr, and you turned out to be the perfect beta reader for this project.

To all my family, friends, and readers, thank you! Sometimes, the love of writing gets drowned out by life, but your encouragement gets me back to my keyboard.

ABRIDGED AUTOBIOGRAPHY

As a second-generation American, I share a love for both my country and for all the places abroad that I haven't seen yet or that I want to see again. It doesn't help that I have enough nationalities mixed into my genetics that I have yet to see all the places my ancestors are from.

I love to read and write almost as much as I love all things Italian–the food, the language, the country, the leather, the coffee, the food, and the list goes on. The slight obsession with Italy is evident in my stories. My preferred schedule is that of a night owl, though I'm adaptable when necessary as long as I have caffeine. When I'm not lost in another world or country, Kansas City is home and the Chiefs are my NFL team.

Jesus is an essential part of my life and identity and a big reason why I keep on writing happy endings. Sometimes I write as a way to balance the power between my imagination and the logical part of my brain, the side that tries to remain tethered to reality.

lbethcampbell.com

For updates on future releases, sign up for my monthly email newsletter through my website and follow me on Instagram

@L.BethCampbell

ALSO BY L. BETH CAMPBELL

At Second Sight

Kissing
the
Blarney
Stone
L. BETH CAMPBELL

The Arranged
Crown
L. BETH CAMPBELL